THE MAN WITH TIGER EYES

KAREN WALLACE

SIMON AND SCHUSTER

SIMON AND SCHUSTER

First published in Great Britain by Simon & Schuster UK Ltd, 2006
A Viacom company

1 3 5 7 9 10 8 6 4 2

Simon & Schuster UK Ltd
Africa House
64–78 Kingsway
London WC2B 6AH

A CIP catalogue record for this book is available from the British Library

ISBN 1 416 90099 3

Typeset by Rowland Phototypesetting Ltd, Bury St Edmunds, Suffolk
Printed by Cox & Wyman, Reading, Berkshire

For Venetia, with love – and thanks

ONE

Lady Violet Winters swung up onto the high chrome bar stool and stared down the length of the shiny white counter. It was the first time she had ever been in a Soda Fountain and she was determined not to make a fool of herself.

Beside her, Garth Hudson, her parent's American ward, leaned forward and grinned.

'So *whaddyawant*?' he asked in his best New York accent. 'How about a chocolate cream soda?'

Violet smiled into Garth's bright brown eyes. Now that she was in New York she realised for the first time that Garth actually *looked* American. His face was sleek and streamlined like the buildings around him. And New York was so different from London. Even the people on the streets walked faster and looked busier. By comparison, London seemed slow and old-fashioned.

It wasn't just the people and the city that were different. Two weeks before, when they had stepped off the ship, Violet's mother, Lady Eleanor, had been wrapped up in her thickest furs. Even Violet had worn her heavy woollen coat with the fox-fur collar and Madame Poisson, her French governess, had hardly been able to move for all the extra layers of flannel petticoats underneath her plain serge skirt. For the first time, she had looked less like her nickname, 'codfish', and more like a whale.

Then, suddenly and annoyingly for Violet, because Garth had predicted it almost to the day, the snow turned to slush and spring exploded over the city. Not a gentle English spring either. Here the sun was hot and flowers appeared out of nowhere. Even the crowds on the streets changed. They grinned as they jostled each other on the sidewalks. It was as if the dark, freezing blanket they had lived under for six months had suddenly been yanked away.

'Huh,' Garth had said when he found Violet sunning herself in the garden of the house her father had rented on Washington Square. 'You wait. There'll be one more blizzard. It always happens.'

And though it seemed impossible in the warm sunshine, Violet believed him. He'd been right about everything else.

Now Violet shifted carefully on her bar stool. She wasn't used to sitting up so high and it would be too embarrassing if she lost her balance. At the far end of the gleaming counter, she could see Madame Poisson was deep in conversation with a woman in a bright stripy apron. That was another extraordinary thing about New York. In certain places, like Soda Fountains, strangers talked to each other. Such familiarity would be unheard of in London.

'So what's happening at the reception we're going to this evening?' asked Violet. She grinned. 'Maybe it'll be the start of another adventure like we had in Cairo last Christmas.'

There was a *clink* on the counter as two tall, wide-necked glasses, brimming with fizzy chocolate and topped with a scoop of ice cream were set in front of them.

'Nah.' Garth slurped up a mouthful of ice cream. 'It's just a reception to show off the portrait painted by that guy I was telling you about.'

'Louis Colbolt?'

Garth nodded. 'I met him when I was a kid.' He swallowed another spoonful of ice cream and let his mind go back to a sunny afternoon when he was seven and Louis and his mother had come to tea. Louis was an art student then and afterwards he had given Garth a pencil sketch of his father. It was the only likeness he had.

Garth dragged his thoughts forward, determined not to get caught up again thinking about his father. Conrad Hudson's strange disappearance in New York the previous year had been on Garth's mind from the moment he had set foot back in his own country. And even though he had become part of Violet's family, Garth knew he had to find out what had happened to his father before he could properly get on with his own life. He looked back at Violet. 'The best thing about this reception is that it's being held in Delmonico's.'

'What's special about that?'

'Delmonico's invented Baked Alaska.'

Violet felt her eyes glaze over as a vision of a crunchy meringue mountain filled with ice cream floated into her mind. Baked Alaska was one of the seven wonders of the world as far as she was concerned.

'So who's going to be at this reception?'

'Everyone who's anyone,' replied Garth in a terrible English accent. 'The Van Horn family are most discerning.'

'About what?'

'About their position in Society, of course! It's their daughter, Daisy, who's the subject of Louis' portrait.' Garth laughed. '*Le tout* New York will be gawping, my dear. You must choose your gown wisely.'

Violet put down her spoon. She knew Garth was only teasing but suddenly she was furious. It was easy for him, he didn't have to put up with her mother. Lady Eleanor was obsessed with appearances and Violet knew she was constantly disappointed in a daughter who did not share her views or indeed inherit her fine-boned face and smooth golden hair. Instead Violet took after her father's side. Her hair was black and curly and her eyes were a deep dark blue but her nose was too long and her mouth was too big.

Violet was handsome rather than pretty.

'What's up?' asked Garth. 'You look like you've swallowed a cactus.'

'My parents will be back from Virginia this afternoon,' said Violet in a miserable voice.

'So?'

'My mother is on the warpath again.'

Garth pulled a face. 'Because of Homer?'

Homer was Violet's pet monkey. She had been given him for Christmas in Egypt and her father had agreed to let him come to New York. Luckily their ship had left England before her mother discovered the fact otherwise Homer would most definitely have been left in the care of the housekeeper in London.

'It's not Homer.' Violet's eyes slid sideways to where Madame Poisson was spooning up her third ice cream. 'She's taken against Madame again.'

Garth knew the scenario. Lady Eleanor wanted a governess with sophistication rather than intelligence. While she knew Violet wanted to follow her father and go to Cambridge, Lady Eleanor still believed that studying at university was a man's hobby, and a governess with social polish would make a better teacher than Madame Poisson. Garth could even hear Lady Eleanor's voice.

That useless French fish! I shall send her home on the next boat!

Garth patted Violet's arm. 'All you have to do is beat your mother at her own game.'

'What do you mean?'

'Ask Madame to help you buy a truly stunning evening dress.' Garth pushed away his empty glass. 'There's a cousin of her brother-in-law who's a *couturier* here.'

'How do you know all this?'

Garth grinned at Violet's long face. 'Eaves-dropping, mostly! Come on, Vi.' He ran a finger across his throat. 'At least you don't have to wear a dumb wing collar that cuts your neck in half.'

'Sometimes I wish I did.'

'Oh, shut up. Your mother will be eating out of your hand if you get it right.'

Before Violet could reply, Garth got up and walked off. 'Give my excuses to Madame! Oh, yeah – and don't buy yellow! I heard some horse-faced hostess say it was common as mustard!'

As Garth disappeared into the street, Madame Poisson bustled over to Violet's side. '*Violette! Where is Garth?*'

Violet slid down from her bar stool and put her hand through her governess's arm. 'Garth asked me to tell you that he has gone back to Washington Square.'

Madame Poisson drew her dark eyebrows together and her popping-out eyes bulged bigger than ever. 'This is most irregular, *Violette*. Did he have a reason?'

Violet smiled into her dear codfish's whiskery face. 'He doesn't like shopping.'

'*Pardon?*'

Violet felt a surge of affection for Garth. He was right. Her mother was always going on about New York fashion. *Always one year behind Paris, darling. Simply impossible not to impress.* Violet felt her jaw tighten. She *would* beat her mother at her own game. 'Madame, will you help me choose a dress for the reception this evening?'

Madame Poisson stared into Violet's startling blue eyes. For a moment there was a silence between them. They both knew the reason for the request.

Madame Poisson squeezed Violet's hand. 'I would be delighted, *ma chère*! Indeed I would be honoured!'

Later that evening, Violet gathered the skirts of her striped cream and purple dress and quietly shut her bedroom door. The folds of heavy silk felt thick and rich in her hand and she ran a finger over the darker plum brocade that edged the high, fitted bodice and long tight sleeves. Her grandmother's cameo brooch gleamed gold at her neck and a pair of amethyst drop earrings shone at her ears.

Madame Poisson had gently swept back her black curly hair and piled it behind her head.

Violette stepped lightly over the carpeted floor and paused at the top of the double marble staircase. In the hall below she could see her father standing with Garth. They both wore formal evening suits with stiff, white collar fronts and cutaway jackets with tails. Lord Percy was speaking as he fiddled with his tie in the huge hall mirror.

'Your friend Louis is tipped to become famous.' He frowned as he pulled his tie too far to one side. 'Ever heard of an art collector called Herbert Wannamaker?'

Violet could see Garth looking unsure. 'He lives in Paris, doesn't he?'

'He does.' Lord Percy pulled his tie in the other direction. 'But he's coming to New York at the end of the month. And if he likes this portrait of Louis', he'll offer him his patronage and a studio in Paris.'

At that moment, Lady Eleanor appeared at the top of the other staircase. She looked over at Violet and a wide smile crossed her face. 'Darling,' she cried in astonishment. 'You look quite, quite beautiful!'

Lady Eleanor rustled across the hall and stood in front of her daughter, who was now almost as tall as she was. 'Where on earth did you find such an exquisite frock?'

Violet looked into her mother's beaming face. 'Madame Poisson chose it for me.'

'Ah, the French!' cried Lady Eleanor as if she had forgotten all about her quarrel with her daughter's governess. 'They have such perfect taste!'

She put her arm through Violet's and the two of them moved smoothly down the wide staircase to the front hall.

'Superb!' said Lord Percy, gazing appreciatively as the two women in his life approached. He held out his hand to his wife and kissed his daughter lightly on the cheek. 'What an honour to accompany you both!'

'Here's to the codfish,' muttered Garth as he helped Violet with her evening cloak. 'I knew she'd pull it off!'

Violet took the woven clasp in her hand and

fixed the cloak around her neck. 'Thanks for the compliment,' she muttered back.

'Any time,' said Garth. 'I'm that kinda guy.'

Violet turned and stuck her tongue out at him. Then she followed her parents out of the front door.

TWO

Delmonico's was a square granite building with a large portico, supported by Roman pillars on either side of wide stone steps. Violet had been there once before with her mother for lunch in the Ladies' Dining Room. It was the first time she had eaten Baked Alaska.

Now everything looked completely different.

Violet walked into an enormous banqueting hall, lined with red silk wallpaper and lit by three glittering crystal chandeliers. The room was packed with people and the air was thick with different perfumes and the smell of pomade. Many of the women wore fashionable, off-the-shoulder dresses with elaborate hairstyles decorated with jewelled sprays and gauzy flowers. Some of the dresses had long trains which moved silkily over the thick Turkish rugs as they walked from group to group.

The first thing that Violet noticed after she became used to the noise, was that the men and women kept to different parts of the room. Often the men stood in circles while the women perched on the edge of ornate gold chairs.

One woman in particular caught Violet's eye. She was large with a heavy masculine face under a pile of curled hair that must have been at least a foot high. Her vast shelf of a bosom was covered in five ropes of pearls and the choker she wore around her neck was wide enough to force her chin upwards so it seemed that she was always staring past the person she was talking to. Her peach satin dress was so tightly fitted that she looked as if she would be unable to stand up without someone propping her at each elbow.

Violet could sense Garth was staring at the same person and the two of them turned quickly away for fear of appearing rude.

'Our hostess, Mrs Enid Van Horn,' murmured Lord Percy. A flicker of a smile crossed his face. 'One of the city's finest monuments, I understand.'

Before either Garth or Violet could reply, Lady Eleanor took them by the arm and led them across the room. 'Come along, my dears. I want to introduce you to Daisy Van Horn.' Lady Eleanor smiled her most beautiful smile, aware that the eyes of most of the room were upon her. 'She's the star of the show, so to speak.'

Ahead of them, standing at the edge of a group of young women and near to a young man, drinking nervously from a large, fluted champagne glass, was Daisy Van Horn. She looked as if she was made out of porcelain. Her lips were perfectly curved under an up-tilted nose and her doll-like eyes seemed painted on her face. As Violet shook her hand, it felt dry and brittle like a bunch of dead twigs. Daisy Van Horn could not have been more different than her overpowering mother in the peach satin gown.

'Daisy, this is my daughter, Violet, and our ward, Garth Hudson.' Lady Eleanor touched the girl lightly on the arm. 'Congratulations, my dear.

15

Everyone is talking about your portrait.'

As her mother spoke, Violet looked at the young man standing next to Daisy. She had never seen such dark hair against such pale skin. She saw the young man start and stare at Garth. He gulped at his glass and stepped forward.

'Garth!'

'Louis!' Garth cried with a big smile. 'Louis Colbolt!'

Violet watched as Daisy Van Horn followed Louis' every move with a tenderness that suddenly brought her face to life. Then she caught Violet's gaze and turned away.

Meanwhile Louis and Garth were laughing and shaking hands.

'You were six,' said Louis.

'Seven,' corrected Garth. 'And you were eighteen.'

'Do you remember my mother?' asked Louis abruptly.

'Of course I do,' replied Garth. 'She gave me the wooden fire engine I played with the afternoon you drew my father's picture.'

For a moment, neither spoke and there was a sadness in Louis' face that Violet couldn't understand. She drew Daisy Van Horn to one side so that Garth and Louis could talk on their own.

'Are you pleased with your portrait?'

'Mother is,' replied Daisy, looking across the room. Violet followed her gaze to where an easel shrouded in a white cloth stood on a raised dais. Daisy swallowed nervously. 'And I'm delighted for Mr Colbolt, of course.' She stared at her feet as if the last sentence had exhausted her.

'My father says an important art collector from Paris is coming especially to see Louis' portrait,' said Violet brightly.

Daisy flushed at the mention of Louis' name. 'Mr Colbolt is a brilliant painter,' she said in a low voice, as if she was repeating a secret. 'Everyone says so.'

A question flashed through Violet's mind. 'Why did your parents choose Louis to paint your portrait? I don't mean to be rude but it wasn't as if he was well-known or anything.'

For the first time, Daisy looked at Violet as if she was actually seeing her. 'Do you know,' she said in the same low voice. 'No one has ever asked me that and *I* wonder, too. The answer is, I have absolutely no idea. One day, my father mentioned it and the next day Lou— I mean, Mr Colbolt, was there.'

Daisy fiddled with a long string of pearls that hung from her neck. 'I got the feeling that Father didn't really care whether I had my portrait painted or not.' She looked sideways at her mother in her peach satin dress. 'And even when it was finished, it was Mama who insisted we held this reception.'

Her voice dropped to a whisper. 'At first Papa refused even to have anything to do with it.' Suddenly she blushed and looked worried and Violet wondered if she was frightened of her father and felt she had betrayed him. At any rate, it was clear she had no great affection for him.

'Gracious,' said Daisy, in a trembling voice. 'I do apologise for my outspokenness, Miss Winters. I don't know what came over me.'

Violet touched Daisy lightly on the wrist. 'Call me Violet. I do hope we will be friends.' As she spoke she found her eyes drawn to the shrouded easel again. 'I can't wait to see your portrait.'

Daisy also turned. The easel looked like a kind of ghostly sculpture at the end of the room. 'Mr Colbolt is the most talented man I have ever met,' she said, proudly.

At that moment, Violet was aware of something the size of a battleship ploughing through the crowded room.

'My dear Daisy,' squawked Enid Van Horn. '*There* you are!'

To Violet's surprise, the huge woman's voice was high and whiney, as if she was speaking through her nose. She nodded to acknowledge Violet's presence, then turned her back on her. Violet felt a violent dislike for Daisy's mother, despite the fact she had never spoken to her.

Enid Van Horn put her vast white hand on Daisy's arm. Her fingers were like white squashy sausages squeezed into jewelled rings. 'I want you to meet Casper Rothman. One of the Boston Rothmans. His mother was at school with me.'

Violet saw Daisy's face fall. She knew only too well from watching women like Enid Van Horn that she was looking for a suitable young man for her daughter to marry. And, judging from the misery that filled Daisy's eyes, her mother had no idea that Louis Colbolt was anything more than a shabbily-dressed young man who happened to have painted her daughter's portrait.

Violet turned away in disgust, vowing to herself, as she vowed time and time again, that she would never marry unless it was to someone she chose herself. As her eyes swept over the room, she saw her mother in her usual place, seated and surrounded by a circle of attentive admirers. That was the extraordinary thing about Lady Eleanor: her beauty and her magnetism defied explanation. Wherever she went, people were drawn to her and fell at her feet. And, just as naturally, Lady Eleanor acknowledged that this was their proper place to be.

On the far side of the room, beside a small table, his face lit by a gold bracket lamp, her father stood talking to a tall, middle-aged man with thin brown hair that hung over his collar. The man had sharp features and a nervous habit of running his fingers along the chain of his pocket watch.

By contrast, Lord Percy looked distinguished and at ease. Violet watched as he leaned forward and smiled, as if the man's conversation was the most interesting he had ever heard.

'That's Philip Van Horn with your father,' said Garth from behind her. 'The mother could knock out a whale, don't you think?'

'Two whales,' muttered Violet. 'And she has no manners, either.'

'Cut you dead, did she?'

'Something like that.' Violet changed the subject. 'Your friend Louis looks miserable.' She grinned mischievously. 'He's in love with Daisy Van Horn, you know.'

'That's crazy,' said Garth. He swallowed the last of his purple grape juice and quickly took another from a silver salver held up by a passing waiter. 'Who told you that?'

Violet touched the side of her nose with her forefinger. 'Female intuition.'

'Balderdash.'

'Bet you!'

'How much?'

'A three-scoop chocolate fudge sundae.' Violet paused. 'My choice of venue.'

Garth narrowed his eyes. 'You're pretty sure of yourself, aren't you?'

'*She's* sweet on *him*, too,' said Violet, ignoring his remark. 'So who knows, maybe the poor painter will marry the pretty heiress and everyone will live happily ever after.'

'It's not funny, Violet,' said Garth, looking suddenly miserable.

Violet stared at him. 'What do you mean?'

'Let's sit down.' Garth turned and threaded his way across to some tables and chairs set out in front of a big window overlooking the street.

Violet hurried after him, aware now that he was upset about something and that her silliness had made it worse.

'What is it, Garth?' she asked anxiously as she sat down across from him. 'What's wrong?'

'Louis's in a terrible fix,' muttered Garth. 'He hasn't got a cent, and two weeks ago his mother wrote to say she had lost all her money in a bad investment.' Garth chewed his lips and tried not to stare at Louis, who was talking animatedly to Lady Eleanor and gulping at another glass of champagne. 'He's pinned everything on this Herbert Wannamaker liking the portrait and taking him on.'

'I don't know much about patrons but I still don't understand how Mr Van Horn found out about Louis in the first place,' said Violet. 'Even Daisy said no one had heard of him.' She looked into Garth's worried face. 'I thought you hardly knew him.'

'I don't, really,' replied Garth. 'It's just that I have good memories of him and his mother.' He paused. 'She was really kind to me and he gave me the only picture I have of my father.'

Violet looked across the room to where Louis was still talking to her mother. Now he was waving his glass in his hand and his face looked even more hectic. 'I agree, something doesn't add up.' She sipped at her fizzy lime drink. 'Tell you what. Let's find out what's going on. It will be our adventure in New York, like the one we had in Egypt.'

Garth snorted. 'There are no criminals in this place. Only a lot of over-stuffed—'

'Shut up,' replied Violet. 'That's just not helpful. From now on, we'll do everything we can to help your friend Louis. Even if it means being nice to that peach-coloured whale in pearls.'

Garth didn't reply. He was staring at the covered easel. Two men in uniform had appeared behind it, half hidden by the long velvet curtains that fell from the ceiling to the floor.

'Garth!' said Violet sharply. 'You haven't listened to a word I've just said.' She followed his gaze. 'Who are those men?'

'Private security guards,' said Garth, frowning. 'They're from Pinkertons. You know, that private detective company I was telling you about.'

'With the motto that says *The Eye Never Closes*?'

'That's them.'

'What would they be doing here?'

'How should I know? Maybe criminals have taken to stealing pearls in broad daylight. There's enough of them here to fill the lake in Central Park.'

At that moment, Philip Van Horn bowed to Lord Percy and crossed over to the dais. At the same time, a man Violet hadn't seen before made his way into the room and walked over to where Louis was standing with Lady Eleanor and Daisy Van Horn. Violet stared at the stranger and for some reason her flesh began to crawl. He was completely different from everyone else in the room. There was something tiger-like about the way he moved and he wore diamond rings on the little fingers of both hands. She saw him bow to her mother and to Daisy, then nod to Louis.

Violet watched her mother intently. What she did next would tell Violet whether this sleek, dangerous-looking man was acceptable in New York Society. Lady Eleanor exchanged the briefest of nods and walked away.

'Garth,' Violet said, standing quickly to her feet. 'A really strange man has just walked up to Daisy and Louis. We must rescue them.'

'What do you mean "rescue"?'

Then Garth saw the man talking to Louis and Daisy and to his astonishment, there was fear in their faces. They looked frozen, like two rabbits caught in the glare of a bright light. 'I'm with you.'

Violet strode up to Daisy and stepped rudely

between her and the man. 'Do excuse me!' she cried in her most upper-class voice. 'I'm from England, you know!' It sounded completely stupid but it was the first thing that came into her mind.

The man stepped back and looked at Violet as if she was a badly behaved child. 'Well now, isn't *that* a coincidence?' he said in a lilting accent. 'I myself am from Ireland. Paul Kelly's the name.'

Violet stared into the man's face. A mocking smile curled around his lips. At first she felt angry that he thought he could look at her in such a dismissive way. Then she found herself staring into his eyes and her stomach shrivelled inside her.

The man's eyes were flecked with gold. Just like a tiger's.

There was a *clink* of a spoon on a glass and a master of ceremonies in a black tailcoat stepped into the middle of the room. 'Pray silence for Mr and Mrs Philip Van Horn.'

Violet watched as Enid and Philip Van Horn swept onto the dais, arm in arm. She was surprised they didn't motion Daisy to join them but one look at Enid Van Horn's face told Violet that this was a moment she had been waiting for and one she intended to keep for herself.

She remembered her mother saying once that Philip Van Horn had trained as an architect in Holland and that when he first came to America, he had had no money to set up his own business. Since his family was respectable, the only solution was to marry an heiress, so he picked Enid Bayard, a plain, overbearing young woman with a huge fortune of her own. Now Violet watched as Enid Van Horn stood as large as the Statue of Liberty. Her chin was thrust upwards and her eyes swept the room like lighthouse flares. They seemed to rest on everyone briefly. Everyone, that is, except her daughter, who still stood frozen to the spot between Louis and the man called Paul Kelly.

'My lords, ladies and gentlemen,' said Philip Van Horn. He turned to his wife and took her hand. 'Enid and I are delighted to present this portrait of our dear daughter, Daisy.' Then, with one smooth movement, he pulled away the white shroud to reveal the painting.

A gasp of amazement went round the room.

Daisy Van Horn's wide, startled eyes stared out of the canvas with an eerie intensity. The smallest of smiles was on her lips. The texture of her skin was almost silver and Louis had painted her against a background of dark, shadowy foliage. Daisy wore a simple white dress with a blood-red sash and held one rose in her hand. Her fine fair hair was pulled back from her face and hung over her shoulders like a shining waterfall.

The effect was extraordinary.

Even though the figure was painted in flesh and blood tones, Daisy Van Horn had the presence of an all-knowing ghost.

Violet watched as the eyes of the crowd turned from the painting to where Daisy stood between Paul Kelly and Louis. A ripple of another kind went through the room but Violet couldn't work out why. Something made her turn quickly to look at Philip Van Horn. His face was dark with fury as he stared at Paul Kelly. He stepped quickly off the dais and spoke urgently to the master of ceremonies. Immediately, waiters went among the crowd with trays full of glasses and the buzz of conversation started up. The merry-go-round of the party was being cranked up again.

'Well, what do you know,' murmured Garth in her ear. 'There's a real live gangster in the room.'

Violet was too busy watching the Pinkerton men step forward as if to protect the painting. 'What on earth is going on?'

'I just told you,' said Garth.

'What?'

Garth raised his eyebrows in an irritating way. 'I beg your pardon, surely?'

'Oh, shut up. What did you just tell me?'

Garth turned to where Daisy had been standing with Louis. 'That man over there . . .' But the man had gone.

'What man?' said Violet impatiently. 'You mean Paul Kelly?'

Garth nodded. 'He's a gangster.'

'*What?* How do you know?'

'Pinkertons' guards. I overheard them talking.'

Violet stared at him. 'Why didn't you tell me?'

Garth rolled his eyes. 'I tried to, but you kept interrupting.'

Across the room, Lord Percy stood talking to Louis Colbolt. He looked up as he heard his daughter's voice. As usual, she was in animated conversation with his ward, Garth. Lord Percy turned back to Louis. Something was bothering him.

'Your mother believes you have a great future, Louis,' said Lord Percy quietly to Louis. 'She told me so in Paris.' He looked again at the painting, which now dominated the room. 'And I agree with her. That portrait is quite brilliant. And that is not a word I use lightly. Indeed, I believe Herbert Wannamaker will offer you his patronage without delay.'

'Thank you, sir,' said Louis, trying to resist the urge to take another glass of champagne from a passing waiter. With the instinct of long service, the waiter stopped and Louis failed in his resolve. He took another glass and gulped its contents.

Then he looked into Lord Percy's kind, thoughtful face and blurted. 'If Mr Wannamaker doesn't take me on, I shall be forced to paint pictures of flowers on chocolate boxes for the rest of my life.'

Lord Percy raised his eyebrows. Surely the young man was exaggerating. Philip Van Horn must have paid him well for the portrait. He opened his mouth to say something, then looked at Louis' flushed face and changed his mind. After all, it was none of his business.

Instead, he took Louis by the arm. 'My wife, Lady Eleanor, whom you have already met, has a fine collection of young painters in London.' He winked at Louis. 'I think perhaps you should meet them one day.'

'Why does Louis look so desperate?' said Violet to Garth. They were both watching as Lord Percy led Louis across the room.

Garth frowned. 'Remember what I told you about his father's problem with the card table?'

'His gambling debts?'

'Exactly.' Garth frowned again. 'Louis is so worried about money. I'm wondering whether he's in the same kind of trouble.'

Violet saw her mother take Louis' hand again and smile. Strangely, she found herself breathing a sigh of relief. Even if he had drunk too many glasses of wine, he had passed her mother's scrutiny with flying colours. And she didn't usually bother to speak to the same person twice at a party. Now Lady Eleanor was drawing Louis away to what looked like a group of old men in fancy waistcoats with big stomachs. Violet smiled to herself. She had to admit that sometimes her mother knew exactly what she was doing.

The rich old men made Violet think of Philip Van Horn. 'Surely Daisy's father has paid Louis for the portrait?'

'I'm sure he did,' said Garth. 'But maybe Louis owed too much money for it to help.'

'Maybe,' repeated Violet. Suddenly she remembered her conversation with Daisy Van Horn and a flutter of excitement went through her. She could feel something wasn't right. 'How can we find out for sure?'

'We'll think of something.' Garth held Violet's eyes. 'Especially now there seems to be a gangster involved.'

Violet felt a thrill of excitement. Their adventure had begun! She was sure of it.

There was the sound of a gong and the master of ceremonies stepped back onto the dais. 'Dinner is served!'

Ten minutes later Violet took her place at a long table covered in a damask cloth overlaid with pale yellow lace. Each setting had at least eight different knives, forks and spoons, with green goblets for Riesling and ruby ones for Claret. Violet heard her mother's voice tutting in her ears. *Green and red glasses. Such a Yankee thing to do.* And Violet had to admit her mother was right. What with the coloured glasses, the be-ribboned arrangements of dyed carnations down the length of the table and the intricately folded yellow napkins, the overall effect was of fairground decorations.

The menu for dinner was laid on a card in front of her. To Violet's delight, she saw Baked Alaska at the bottom; though there were four other courses to get through first. She peered at the card again. Oysters with sherry bitters came first, followed by clear green turtle soup. Violet didn't mind oysters and she liked turtle soup because it was served in pretty turtle-shaped china bowls with domed lids to keep the soup hot. She looked at the menu again.

Canvas back duck with hominy and redcurrant jelly.

Saddle of lamb à la sauce Bernaise.

Violet pulled a face. How would she ever get through all of this and still have room for a helping of Baked Alaska?

A young man with slicked-back hair and a straight side parting sat down beside her. He held out his hand.

'Cecil Heinzburger.'

Violet racked her brain to remember why his name was familiar. Then, just before it became embarrassing, the answer came to her. He was the fiancé of Henrietta Wortley who she and Garth had met in Cairo last Christmas.

Violet held out her hand. 'Congratulations on your engagement, Mr Heinzburger.'

Cecil smiled. He had a beaky nose and a receding chin but there was a gleam in his eye and Violet liked the look of him. 'Miss Wortley, I mean, Henrietta and I are delighted.' He spread his napkin over his knees. 'She speaks so highly of you. Do tell me how you met.'

34

As Violet described the wonderful hotel they had stayed at in Cairo, she remembered clearly Henrietta's nervous horse-like face bent over old editions of the *Illustrated London News*, sitting on the verandah, while her battle-axe of a mother dominated the room with a voice as loud as cannon fire. Violet had been delighted when she heard that Henrietta had found an escape in Cecil Heinzburger.

'Now, it's your turn,' said Violet, smiling. 'How did *you* and Henrietta meet?'

'On board the *Lara*, on my way back to Paris,' said Cecil, blushing. 'I joined it at Suez.'

'Good grief,' cried Violet. 'That was the steamer we took out to Alexandria!'

She leaned to her right as a waiter set down an oyster plate in front of her. Five oysters were arranged around a central well filled with sherry bitters. Violet stared at the pearly white insides of the shells. On the other side of the table, a few seats up, she saw Garth's face drop like a stone. If there was one thing he hated, it was oysters.

Garth looked up, feeling her stare. He rolled his

eyes once and went back to talking to Henrietta Wortley, who had been seated beside him.

Violet smiled to herself. She had never known such a fussy eater as Garth. If he had his own way, he would happily live on peas and custard. She cast her eye across the row of forks and picked one with a long, narrow stem and four prongs cut into a circle of silver.

At the other end of the row was the ice-cream fork which, as far as Violet was concerned, was the most important fork on the table.

Violet lifted her oyster expertly out of its shell and turned back to Cecil Heinzburger. 'Tell me about your America.'

'*My* America, Lady Violet?' Henrietta's fiancé dipped his own oyster in the pool of sherry bitters. 'My America is about canned meat.'

'Canned meat?'

'That's my family business,' replied Cecil, proudly. He leaned towards her and spoke quietly. 'And do you know what?'

'What?' said Violet, for the third time that night.

Cecil straightened up, speared another oyster

and looked her full in the face. 'I'm going to be the Canned Meat King of this country!'

Two hours later, Violet knew more about the refrigeration and canning of meat than she would have thought possible or, indeed, desirable; but at least it had given her a chance to think her own thoughts as Cecil talked on and on.

She found her eyes resting on Philip Van Horn, who was sitting across from Garth. As course followed course, he had eaten with little or no enthusiasm. Indeed, Violet had the strong impression that he wanted nothing more than to get away from the room as soon as was decently possible. She remembered the look of fury on his face when he saw Paul Kelly and even though Kelly had left soon after, his mood obviously hadn't changed.

Beside him, a stick insect of a woman in a rose-pink organza dress, cut low over her scrawny chest, pecked at her food like a chicken. Violet had watched her try to talk to Philip Van Horn time and time again but every attempt had failed. On his other side, an elderly lady wearing a tiara must have given up on him ages ago. She was shovelling her food into her mouth with single-minded gusto.

Finally the moment Violet had been waiting for arrived. A dozen waiters, each carrying a huge silver salver covered with a high silver dome, walked in a procession down the sides of the room. At a signal from the head waiter, they all lifted up the silver domes and put them on the sideboards behind them.

Violet could have clapped her hands as twelve snowy mountains of crunchy meringue appeared in a row in front of her.

Cecil Heinzburger wiped his mouth with his napkin. 'Baked Alaska is my favourite food.' His voice dropped to a whisper. 'After Heinzburger's canned meat, of course.'

'Of course,' agreed Violet, but she was watching the master of ceremonies cross the room to Philip Van Horn. The man was walking quickly and his face looked grey and shocked. He bent down and whispered in Philip Van Horn's ear.

By now everyone was watching and the long table had gone silent.

'Stolen?' The word exploded from Philip Van Horn's mouth like gunshot. 'What do you mean, *stolen*?'

There was a *crash* as a chair hit the floor.

Louis Colbolt threw down his yellow napkin and ran from the table.

A second later, a howl of anguish echoed around the next door room and there was a loud *bang* as a door slammed shut.

THREE

Lady Eleanor snapped her newspaper shut and dropped it on the breakfast table. 'I've never read such rubbish in all of my life,' she said in a cross voice. 'Really, these American newspapers will print anything. I hope Philip sues them.'

Lord Percy lifted his cup of coffee to his lips and drank thoughtfully. 'Even *you* must admit it's an odd state of affairs,' he said, returning the cup to its saucer.

'Odd?' repeated Lady Eleanor. 'It's absolutely outrageous!'

'You misunderstand, dear,' said Lord Percy, who had been surprised enough to see his wife up before mid morning and was now even more surprised to see her so excitable. Then again, Lady Eleanor had strong views on discretion, and American news reporting was far from subtle.

'You must agree,' said Lord Percy, 'that it is rather strange to invite a known gangster to a reception celebrating the unveiling of your daughter's portrait.'

He drank more coffee. 'Of course, Philip's affairs are his own business.'

Violet looked up from her waffles. There was something in her father's voice which made her wonder if he knew more about Philip Van Horn than he was letting on. She kicked Garth under the table.

Garth replied with the briefest of nods.

'The most terrible thing is the disappearance of Louis Colbolt,' cried Lady Eleanor. She picked up her paper and shook it open again. 'It says here that the Police Department have already carried out a search of the harbour front and they're planning to drag the river today.'

'Louis won't have thrown himself off a bridge,' insisted Garth, almost angrily. 'I'm sure of it.'

'Calm yourselves,' said Lord Percy quietly. 'It's normal procedure for the police to drag the river when someone has disappeared.'

Violet put down her knife and fork and folded her napkin. As far as she was concerned, breakfast was over. She had been waiting for this moment since the night before, when she had seen Garth run from the chaotic banqueting hall. In the confusion, no one but her had noticed him slip out of the reception-room door. Twenty minutes later, he had appeared at her side.

'I saw him,' Garth had whispered breathlessly. 'He was talking to—'

Then Lord Percy and Lady Eleanor had come towards them.

'Keep them talking,' Violet had said quickly. She had run over to where Daisy Van Horn was standing, white and rigid beside her mother, and whispered quickly in her ear. 'If you ever need help, you can trust Garth and me. Come to Washington Square.'

Before Daisy could reply, her mother had circled her arm with giant white fingers and dragged her away. 'For heaven's sake, girl! Pull yourself together!'

Now Violet pressed her breakfast napkin to her lips. 'May I get down, Mama?'

'Of course, my dear,' replied Lady Eleanor. 'I'm sorry the conversation this morning was so, ah, upsetting.' She smiled and held up her cheek for Violet to kiss. 'Will you have lessons now?'

'No,' said Violet.

'Yes,' said Garth.

'Surely Madame Poisson has arranged something?' said Lady Eleanor in a puzzled voice.

'Oh, yes, Mama,' said Violet smoothly. 'We are learning about modern architecture today.' She smiled at her father. 'First hand!'

'Perfect weather for study,' said Lord Percy, lifting his newspaper in front of his face.

Lady Eleanor frowned but before she could ask any awkward questions, Violet and Garth had said their good mornings and walked into the front hall.

As soon as Violet had shut the door behind them, she turned to Garth. 'So, what happened?' she whispered quickly. 'I haven't slept a wink all night.'

'That makes two of us,' said Garth. He flung on a jacket. 'Come on. Let's get some air before shark snout comes down.'

'It's codfish, thick head,' said Violet as she pulled her tartan cloak around her shoulders. 'When are you going to get it right?'

Garth rolled his eyes and opened the French doors at the end of the hall. 'Maybe never.'

A faint spring breeze was in the air as Violet and Garth made their way down the gravel path into the garden. Violet was astonished. White and yellow crocuses had appeared in the grass almost overnight. They headed for a bench that was hidden from the house behind a clipped yew hedge. From there they could see through high, wrought-iron railings and watch passers-by on the street.

As usual everyone was in a hurry. Even women out shopping didn't dawdle and chatter like they did in London.

'So, what happened?' said Violet again. 'What did you see?' She sat down on the bench and stared as two young ladies in day dresses and long, flowing coats walked purposefully down the road.

'It was most peculiar,' replied Garth. He looked into Violet's serious dark eyes. 'Something strange is going on, that's for sure.'

'Then just as well we're here to find out what it is,' said Violet crisply. She patted the bench. 'Now, stop walking up and down like some demented lion and tell me what happened – *from the beginning.*'

Garth grinned at the edge in her voice. 'Sorry. I must be driving you nuts.'

'You are.'

'OK. When I got down to the front steps, there was no sign of Louis at all. I took a guess and turned left. Then I ran as fast as I could.' Garth paused. 'I was lucky. I saw a shiny new cab in a side street and there he was, talking to that gangster.'

'Paul Kelly.'

Louis nodded. In his mind's eye, he saw himself edge towards the two men in the shadow of a high brick wall. He knew he had to stop before he came too close to the pool of light from the next lamp, otherwise they would see him. However, the street was quiet and Garth could hear Louis' voice clearly.

He was shouting. 'Give me back my painting! I'll pay you! I promise I'll pay you!'

'So maybe we were right about the gambling debts,' said Violet in a thoughtful voice. 'What did Kelly say?'

Garth pulled a face. 'Louis was yelling so much it was difficult to hear. Kelly was speaking all right, but quietly, as if nothing out of the ordinary was happening.'

Violet looked up sharply. 'Didn't you hear *anything* we could go on?'

Garth nodded. 'I saw Kelly put his hand on Louis' arm. Then he said, "It's your choice, Louis. You're the artist. You'll get your painting back. All I need is a little help with a camel-hair brush."'

Garth turned to Violet. 'Then Louis yelled, "You're a crook! If I do what you want I'll be a crook, too!" And Kelly just smiled.' Garth shook his head. 'I could see his face in the light. He *smiled*! Then he leaned forward and said, "I hear your mother isn't well."'

At that point Garth got up from the bench and began pacing back and forth again. When he spoke his voice was raw and furious. 'Louis started sobbing. Kelly opened the door to his cab and—'

'Louis got in,' said Violet flatly.

Garth nodded. 'Violet! We've got to help him! He's obviously in dreadful trouble!'

'Do you think we should tell my father?' asked Violet.

Garth shook his head. 'I was thinking that, but your father doesn't really know Louis and he wouldn't think much of him if he found out he had gambling debts. He might even feel obliged to warn Herbert Wannamaker.'

'*Violette! Violette!*' Amelie Poisson's voice sounded high and agitated. 'Where are you?'

Garth put his head in his hands. 'Get rid of her.'

Violet jumped up from the bench as the little French governess came rushing down the gravel path.

'*Madame!*' cried Violet. 'Whatever is the matter?'

'You must come quickly,' cried Madame Poisson breathlessly. 'It is Homer. He—'

Violet turned to Garth and he shrugged. He knew

she was devoted to Homer and that the monkey would come first.

'What's happened to him?' cried Violet.

'Nothing's the matter with *'im*!' cried Madame Poisson, almost hysterically. 'It is the curtains he is ripping. They are in shreds and the maid cannot catch him!'

Violet burst out laughing. It was more from relief than anything else.

'Don't laugh, *Violette,*' cried Madame Poisson. 'If Lady Eleanor sees him . . .' The little French woman drew a line across her throat with a finger. 'No one can save him this time.'

'Where is he?' asked Violet, suddenly nervous.

'In the drawing room,' replied Madame Poisson in a hollow voice.

'Oh, no!' cried Violet, understanding for the first time the real danger. 'Who let him go?'

'Nobody let him go, you silly child,' snapped Madame Poisson. 'He opened his cage door!' She looked at her watch. 'And you have two minutes to catch him before your mother's visitor, Mrs Stuyvesant Fish—'

Violet didn't hear any more. She was already up the path and heading in the back door.

Dottie, the maid, was shaking all over and waving a feather duster in the air. 'Miss! Miss! He's on the curtain rail, Miss! And he's got ... he's got ...'

'He's got *what*?' cried Violet, impatiently. At the top of the spiral staircase, she could hear her mother giving instructions to a servant.

'One of those fancy china eggs,' said the maid, helplessly.

Violet's face went white. The only fancy china eggs in the drawing room were priceless Russian antiques. She ran down the corridor and pulled open the panelled door.

It was worse than she had thought. Homer didn't just have one Fabergé egg, he had two. He was hanging upside down by his tail from the curtain pole with one in each paw.

'Homer!' said Violet in a firm voice. 'Put down those eggs right now!'

The tiny brown-haired monkey glared at her and

held out the eggs as if he was about to take her at her word and drop them.

'No!' said Violet sharply. 'Come here and put them in my hands!' She stood underneath him and held out her hands.

Homer's eyes softened and he looked as if he was considering her request. He made a small chirruping noise and moved carefully along the rail towards the curtain.

Outside, there was the clatter of wheels on cobblestones and then a *creak* as the main gates were opened. Violet looked out the window and saw a short, imperious-looking woman step down from a cab.

It could only be Mrs Stuyvesant Fish.

At the sound of the gates, Homer had stopped moving.

'Homer,' pleaded Violet, as if he could understand every word she said. 'If you don't come down now, Mama will send you away and I won't be able to stop her.'

The monkey cocked his head. But he still didn't move.

'I know you've been shut inside and I know you don't like it,' said Violet in a conversational voice, though inside she was screaming, 'but Homer, the only reason I've left you behind is because it's been so cold.' She pointed out of the window. 'It's a lovely spring day now. I thought we might go for a walk.'

That was it. Homer made his way quickly down the curtain and put the two priceless jewelled eggs in Violet's hands. Then he clambered up onto her shoulder and nuzzled her ear with his furry face.

Violet just had time to put the eggs back in their stands when the door opened and Mrs Stuyvesant Fish was shown into the room.

'Oh, my dear!' she cried. Her face softened and all her imperiousness vanished at the sight of the monkey pressed close to Violet's cheek. 'He's a talapoin, isn't he?'

Violet nodded. No grown-up had ever shown any interest in Homer before, let alone known what breed he was.

Mrs Stuyvesant Fish's round face beamed. 'Why, I do envy you children today! Last weekend I visited

51

the Roosevelts in the White House and young Ted –
he's the oldest boy, you know – had *such* a gorgeous
macaw on his shoulder.' She chuckled and tickled
Homer's chin. 'His father said it had a bill that could
bite through an iron boiler plate.'

'Lady Eleanor will be with you presently,' said
Dottie, bobbing at the door. She didn't dare look
inside the room.

'Thank you.' Mrs Stuyvesant Fish saw the look of
panic on Violet's face and chuckled again. 'You run
along, dear. Perhaps we'll meet another time!' As
she spoke, she reached over and turned the Fabergé
eggs the right way up.

Violet threw her a grateful smile and ran from
the room.

Daisy Van Horn clutched the rag doll her grandmother had given her when she was six and rocked
back and forth on her bedroom floor. She felt
her heart would break. All she could think about
was Louis' pale face, floating just under the murky
waters of the East River. She was *sure* he had
thrown himself off a bridge.

Tears ran down Daisy's white face. She hadn't slept for worrying. Every time she closed her eyes, she heard his voice choked with anger and despair. *They don't understand. They just don't understand.*

Daisy groaned and clutched her doll more closely. She could see everything as if it was happening around her at that very moment. There was Louis, gulping glass after glass of champagne and every time someone came up to congratulate him, he had hung his head and muttered at them. The only person he seemed easy with was Lady Eleanor Winters, then, as soon as she had left, he went back to drinking on his own. Daisy heard herself asking why he was so upset, when tonight was supposed to be a celebration. It was then that Louis had turned on her.

'How can I celebrate when my mother is sick and I'm too broke to cable her a cent?'

Daisy remembered staring at him. What on earth was he talking about? She knew perfectly well that her father had paid him a good fee for the portrait. She'd heard him say as much to her mother. But when she told Louis this, he had only stared at her with red, glassy eyes. Then he gulped down another glass and told her that no matter what she had heard her father say, he had not paid him any money, despite Louis having repeatedly asked for something, anything – even if it wasn't the full payment.

'Every time I remind him, your father pretends he's forgotten,' Louis had said bitterly. 'He promises to mail me a cheque.' More champagne went down his throat. *Nothing.*'

Daisy had been aghast. Yet she had a horrible feeling that Louis was telling the truth.

A great sob rose in her throat and now she buried her face in the doll's faded gingham apron. *Nothing.* That was the last word she had heard her dear Louis say.

Downstairs a door slammed and her father's angry voice rose up the stairwell. 'It was all your idea, Enid,' he shouted. 'I never wanted the damned reception in the first place!'

'I didn't invite a known gangster!' screamed her mother. Something smashed. '*Everyone* knows Paul Kelly runs gambling houses.'

'I didn't invite him *either*!' roared her father.

'Then why was he there?' Another *smash*.

'How should I know? I've never seen him before!'

Daisy's head went cold and fizzy and she rolled up in a ball on the floor. It was the first time in her life she had heard her father tell a deliberate lie and it was a huge one. He *did* know Paul Kelly. She had seen them together only a month before.

Daisy's mind went back to that cold February day. She had taken a cab all the way down Broadway to walk across Brooklyn Bridge. She was fascinated by bridges and this was the first suspension bridge she had ever seen. Every week while it was being built she had joined a crowd of spectators who watched in amazement as teams of workmen fixed the huge granite pillars into the riverbed. All of New York agreed it was nothing short of a miracle.

Now that the bridge was finished, Daisy made a point of paying a cent to walk across the East River whenever she could find the time.

She saw herself staring out of her cab window. They were stuck behind a brewer's wagon in the Bowery district. Daisy shuddered at the memory.

The Bowery was a rough part of town, full of tenement blocks, stuffed to bursting with poor immigrant families. She found herself staring at the crowds of ragged people with hungry faces, trying to imagine what their lives must be like. It was impossible.

Suddenly her father had appeared in a hotel doorway, with a strange man beside him. The man was dressed in a well-cut double-breasted jacket. He wore a cravat and carried a gold-topped cane. But even from her cab, Daisy could sense there was something dangerous about him.

But it was the expression on her father's face that Daisy remembered so clearly. He had looked hunted and desperate.

All Daisy's life, her father had made it his business to be in control. He held his chin high and the firm line of his jaw told everyone around him he was the boss. Yet when Daisy had seen him beside Paul Kelly, he had looked beaten. Then the gangster had held out his hand and her father had turned abruptly away.

At that point, her own cab had jolted forwards.

But not before Daisy saw Paul Kelly stare after her father's retreating figure and allow a triumphant, mocking smile to spread across his face.

A floor below, the heavy front door slammed. Daisy stood up and looked out of her window. Her father was climbing into a cab. His face was black and furious. Questions crashed around Daisy's head.

What was Paul Kelly doing at her reception?

Why had Louis been so afraid of him?

Why did her father lie about him?

What on earth was going on?

Daisy threw herself onto her bed and sobbed.

FOUR

Philip Van Horn stared at his gloved hands. It was as if they belonged to someone else. They kept clenching and unclenching themselves into fists on his lap. For the first time in his life, he felt the foundations of his world disintegrating.

'Damn him,' muttered Philip Van Horn. 'Damn Paul Kelly to hell.' But even as he spat out the words like bits of bad meat, he was sure that Paul Kelly would be in no rush to go anywhere. Least of all hell. And as Philip Van Horn knew only too well, what Paul Kelly wanted, Paul Kelly got.

A noise halfway between a groan and a snarl escaped from his mouth. Of course he knew what sort of man Paul Kelly was. Thirty years ago they had been in business together. But it hadn't been the sort of business Philip Van Horn practised now. Where a gentleman's word was his bond. Where everyone was respectable. Where keeping up appearances mattered more than anything else.

As the cab jostled through the traffic down Fifth Avenue, Philip Van Horn looked out at the square brownstone mansions of Vanderbilt Row, at the University Club of which he was a member and at the brand new Plaza Hotel. *This* was his world now. No one would ever know that once he had been nothing but a poor architect with only one good suit and a battered leather Gladstone bag to his name. Then he had walked down Fifth Avenue and promised himself that one day he would mix with the Goulds and the Astors and the Stokes. That one day he would be elected to the University Club and drink cocktails with New York's High Society. And Philip Van Horn had achieved what he wanted. Even though it had been with the help of Paul Kelly, whose thugs forced out the people who lived in the big houses on the East Side so that he and Van Horn could buy them cheap and convert them into tenement buildings. The rent from fifty families living in cramped, stinking conditions had made Kelly and Van Horn a fortune.

At the time, the arrangement had suited both men. Van Horn had respectability but needed the money. And, once he got it, he set about courting Enid Bayard.

Paul Kelly, on the other hand, never cared about respectability. He was in the tenement business for money and power. By the time the two men went their own ways, Paul Kelly was the undisputed leader of the Bowery underworld and had a finger in every gambling racket on the East Side of the city. When they shared out the last of their profits, the two men didn't even shake hands. Paul Kelly had walked out of Philip Van Horn's life with the promise that he would never return.

But he had broken that promise.

As Philip Van Horn's cab rattled past the still leafless trees of Central Park, he felt his stomach shrink at the memory. A month earlier Paul Kelly had come up to him outside the Athenaeum Club.

'Got time for a drink with an old friend?' Kelly had said, smiling. He was dressed as elegantly as ever in a felt Homburg hat and a racing green three-piece suit. It was cold and his heavy overcoat had a glossy beaver-skin collar.

For a split second, Philip Van Horn hadn't moved or spoken. He had been too horrified to do either, but he knew he could not risk any kind of public disagreement.

'Come on, now,' said Paul Kelly in a coaxing voice, as he placed his gloved hand on Philip's arm. 'Surely a wander down memory lane would be a fine thing after all these years?'

'Take your hand off me.' Philip Van Horn's voice had been no more than a harsh whisper. 'We've got nothing to say to each other.'

'Ah, but that's where you're wrong.' Paul Kelly had tightened his grip on Philip's arm and led him over to a waiting cab. 'I've got rather a lot to say to you and, if you want to keep your fancy friends, I'd suggest you listen.'

Their cab had stopped outside a hotel on Broadway, down in the Bowery. It was called the

Silver Dollar and Philip Van Horn remembered it from thirty years before.

They had walked through a dingy hall with faded plush wallpaper and flaking gold-painted lamp brackets. All the way there, Philip Van Horn had refused to speak so Paul Kelly had done the talking. It didn't seem to matter to him whether his ex-partner was listening or not. His smooth, caramel voice swirled around the cab like so much scented smoke. He wasn't asking much. Just a favour for old time's sake. All Philip Van Horn had to do was commission a portrait. It didn't matter whose. It could be a dog's for all Kelly cared. But the painter had to be a young man called Louis Colbolt and Philip Van Horn was to offer him a thousand dollars and then not pay him.

Kelly had opened a wooden door on the far side of the hotel lobby. The office beyond had a huge mahogany desk at one end and a brightly burning fire at the other. Two button-back leather sofas stood on either side of a carved mantelpiece. The sideboard glistened with cut-glass decanters and silver trays.

'Drink?' Paul Kelly asked, pouring himself a tumbler of bourbon.

'No,' snapped Philip Van Horn, watching the gangster's footsteps. Kelly moved as noiselessly as a tiger. He always had done.

Suddenly Van Horn's temper exploded. 'How dare you accost me outside my own club?' He glared at Kelly's half-closed yellow eyes. 'You promised to stay out of my life. That was the deal.'

Paul Kelly shrugged. 'I'm no gentleman.' He sipped at his bourbon. 'Never pretended I was. So you see, I've got nothing to lose.' He smiled. 'You have everything.' He turned back to the sideboard. 'Sure you won't change your mind?'

'You disgust me,' snarled Philip Van Horn.

'Strong words for a criminal,' said Kelly. He poured out another bourbon and held it out. Van Horn took it and gulped at it.

'All right,' he said angrily. 'I'll do what you ask but I don't want to know why.' He finished the drink and put the glass on the sideboard. 'In return, I never want to see you again.'

He opened the door and started down the

corridor into the hotel lobby. Paul Kelly quickly caught up with him and the two men walked out together onto the busy sidewalk. It was a bright February morning and the street was clogged with traffic.

Paul Kelly smiled and his yellow eyes glittered. 'You have my promise.' A hansom cab clattered past. Paul Kelly held out his hand. 'A gentleman's word.'

'Sewer rat,' croaked Philip Van Horn, but he knew he was beaten. He turned on his heel and walked quickly away.

The hansom cab jerked forward into the traffic. As Philip Van Horn pushed into the crowd he kept his eyes on his feet. If he'd looked up he would have stared straight into the eyes of his daughter, Daisy.

Now, as his own cab rattled past Central Park, Philip Van Horn's hands clenched and unclenched as he remembered the smug look on Kelly's face at the reception. 'I'll kill him,' he muttered. 'I swear I'll kill him.'

The cab stopped and the driver peered at him. 'Beg your pardon, Mister Horn?'

'Nothing. Drive on, Sidney. I'm in a hurry.'

'Yessir.' Sidney Nolan drew his eyebrows together. It had been the talk of the kitchen when the housekeeper read out the morning papers. Why, it put a respectable house to shame. What was a gangster doing at a Van Horn reception?

Sidney Nolan shook his head and whipped the horse forward. That morning, he'd been waiting for his orders by the front door as usual. He couldn't help hearing the master and mistress fighting like a pair of common alley cats.

What was the world coming to?

If Philip Van Horn had known how furious he looked as he stared out his cab window, he might have thought to draw the curtains. As it was, when Garth and Violet stepped onto the sidewalk from the library, Violet found herself staring at the same angry face she had seen the night before.

'Garth!' cried Violet. 'Over there! The cream-coloured cab! It's Philip Van Horn!'

'Good grief,' muttered Garth. 'He looks as if he wants to kill someone!'

'Blast!' cried Violet. 'I wish we could follow him!'

But it was impossible. Madame Poisson had come with them to the library and was still inside, reading up on the history of sewing machines.

Garth only shrugged. He had spent the morning studying newspaper clippings, looking for stories about his father's disappearance. He'd found nothing and now he could barely hide his disappointment.

As Philip Van Horn's cab pulled away, an idea flashed into Violet's mind. 'Let's go back to the library,' she said to Garth.

'What for? You didn't find anything about Kelly.'

'But I'm still sure there's some connection between Van Horn and Paul Kelly.'

'So?'

'So, I was looking at stories about Kelly,' said Violet carefully. 'Maybe I should try from the other side.'

'You mean, Van Horn?'

Violet nodded. 'Why not? There's nothing to lose. The codfish will be there for at least another twenty minutes.' She looked into Garth's unhappy face. 'We might even find something about your father. He must have known Philip Van Horn.'

'OK.' Garth turned and they walked back up the steps and went through the library doors.

FIVE

'I think you should take up the barrel organ,' said Garth to Violet as they walked up Fifth Avenue on either side of Madame Poisson.

'Why should I?' asked Violet, stroking Homer's fur through his red felt jacket.

Garth grinned. 'You'd make a fortune.' He turned and pointed to a huge mansion that looked like a castle. 'Just like Cornelius Vanderbilt here. Do you know he spent five million dollars on this house alone? *And* he's got three more like it.'

Madame Poisson snorted dismissively. 'Money cannot buy good taste, Garth.' She waved a gloved hand at the fussy, carved stonework and the footmen in livery standing by the front door. '*Poof!* This is ridiculous. 'Ee is nothing but a rich *businessman.*'

Garth laughed. 'That counts for everything in this city, Madame. Some people would kill to get through that front door.'

Violet tossed her head. 'I've had quite enough of fat men with fat wallets and fat women boasting about their pearls!' She quickened her step. 'Look – there's Central Park! Let's see the ice-skating lake!'

'Too late,' replied Garth. 'It's melted.'

Violet's face fell.

'Maybe it'll freeze over again,' said Garth, kindly. 'Remember, there's still a blizzard to come.'

Madame Poisson's button eyes twinkled. '*That* would keep your Homer inside, *Violette!*'

'Madame!' protested Violet. 'You sound as if you would be pleased.' She tickled the little monkey's chin. 'Poor Homer! Nobody loves you but me!'

A fire truck rattled by with its bell clanging loudly. In that instant, Violet remembered she hadn't fastened Homer's leash to her belt. She reached up to grab it.

Too late!

Homer let out a terrified screech and jumped from her shoulder into the street, dragging his leash behind him.

'Homer!' screamed Violet at the top of her voice. 'Garth! Quick! Catch him! He'll get run over!'

Garth was about to dash after him when he felt a hard tug on his jacket.

'Idiot!' Madame Poisson's voice was sharp and angry. 'You'll get yourself killed chasing that monkey! Don't you dare go after him!'

'But *Madame*!' wailed Violet. Homer had disappeared in the chaos of wheels and horses' hooves that jammed the wide street in front of them. 'He'll be run over! I know he will!'

She ran up and down the sidewalk, peering into the traffic. There was no sign of Homer anywhere. At first she couldn't believe what had happened. Then, as moments passed and she still couldn't see him, a great sob grabbed at Violet's throat and she threw herself down on a street bench and buried her face in her hands.

'Is dis munkey anyting to do with you, lady?'

Through streaming eyes, Violet saw a skinny boy standing in front of her. His clothes were ragged and his face was grimy but Homer was in his arms. She stared stupidly at the boy, unable to speak for relief and joy.

'Lady,' said the boy, sharply. 'I'm askin' yus twice. Is dis your munkey?'

Violet nodded. She hadn't heard such a thick Irish accent for a long time. 'Yes,' she said in a shaky voice. She held out her arms and Homer leaped onto her shoulder and pressed his shivering face hard against her ear. 'Thank you.'

'Mickey Gallagher's de name. Pleased to meet yer.'

Violet found herself grasping a small bony hand. 'Thank you,' she said again. 'Please, let me give you some money.'

The boy grinned. 'Now dere's a notion I'd be happy with.'

Madame Poisson ran up to them. '*Violette!*' she cried breathlessly. '*Vraiment!* We thought we'd lost you!' She stared at Homer, who was still glued to Violet's neck. 'And 'ere you are and 'ere is Homer, too!'

Mickey turned to Violet with wide-open eyes. 'She ain't Oirish, is she?'

Violet laughed before she could stop herself.

'I don't see what's so funny,' snapped Madame Poisson. 'You rush into the crowd. Garth and I can't see you anywhere.' The little French woman's face flushed with irritation. 'And now you laugh at me!'

'Yus got it all wrong, Lady,' said Mickey in a solemn voice. 'She ain't laughin' at yus. She's only laughin', if yus understand my meanin'.'

Violet stood up. 'Madame Poisson, may I present Master Mickey Gallagher. He very kindly rescued Homer and I would like to give him a reward.'

'A big one at dat,' added Mickey quickly.

Something about the grimy little urchin went straight to Madame Poisson's heart. When she thought about it later, she couldn't explain why. The streets were full of them. And they'd as soon pick your pocket as risk their lives chasing after monkeys. She held out her hand and shook Mickey's dirty fingers. She smiled and gave him a dollar bill. 'You 'ave saved our day,' she said. 'What would we 'ave done without you?'

To his amazement, Mickey felt a blush creeping up his neck. 'Ah, don' take me for no saint, lady.' He turned and patted Homer's tail. 'Any of us boys woulda chased after him.'

'Perhaps,' said Madame Poisson. 'But they would 'ave run off with him, too.'

Mickey shifted from foot to foot. He wasn't used to people saying nice things to him. It made him feel uncomfortable. 'Ah, shut your mouf, lady,' he muttered under his breath.

Violet gasped. Behind her, Garth smothered his own laughter. He had only heard the last exchange and waited for Madame Poisson to lose her legendary temper and clout the street kid over the head with her umbrella.

Instead, Garth was astonished.

'*Ooh là là*, Mickey!' replied Madame Poisson, smiling. 'I don't think that is the way to carry on at all!'

Mickey looked into Madame Poisson's face. It was oval, and her eyes seemed to pop out on either side. For some reason, she reminded Mickey of a fish. But a nice fish. In Mickey's books, whoever gave him money was always nice.

'Dat monkey should be in a cage, Miss,' he said, turning to Violet. 'Yus was lucky this time. I didn't catch him. He jumped onto me!'

At this point Garth stepped forward. He'd never shaken hands with a street kid but since everyone else had, he wanted to as well. 'Garth Hudson.'

'Mickey Gallagher.' Mickey jerked his head at Homer. 'Dat monkey should be in a cage,' he said again.

'Don't tell me,' said Garth. 'Tell her.'

Mickey looked at the group of people around him. The big kid was American but the other two talked funny. At any rate, they certainly didn't come from New York. Not much passed by Mickey but even he couldn't work out how they all fitted together. The boy called Garth and the girl called Violet certainly weren't brother and sister and the little fish woman wasn't their mother. Mickey took in the good clothes and polished leather boots. Whoever they were, they had money. And that was what mattered to him. He took a gamble.

'I could help yus with a cage,' he said quickly. 'And get yus a good price, too.' Mickey paused and picked on Violet. 'I knows the best pet store in the city, see.'

Violet was so relieved to have Homer back safe and sound that she would have agreed to anything.

Madame Poisson also saw her chance. She had anticipated an argument about finding a really secure cage for Homer. But thanks to Mickey, it looked as if she was going to succeed after all. 'That's very kind of you, Mickey,' she said. 'We would be extremely obliged if you would take us there.'

'Where is it?' asked Garth. Unlike Violet and her governess, he had not fallen under the spell of this Irish urchin.

Mickey saw immediately that Garth was his problem. 'Tenth Street,' he said reluctantly. 'That's in the Bowery.'

'I know where it is,' said Garth. He drew his eyebrows together. 'I'm not sure—'

'If you're thinking it's too rough for me, don't

bother,' said Violet in a irritated voice. Like Madame Poisson, she had been charmed by Mickey. She turned to Garth. 'Anyway, I read in those newspaper clippings that that's where Paul Kelly comes from. I'd like to go there.'

'Who is this Paul Kelly?' asked Madame Poisson. She had been up very early that morning and had missed out on the talk in the kitchen.

Violet didn't reply. She was staring at Mickey's face. It had gone white. 'I didn't say nuffin' about Paul Kelly,' said Mickey. 'This is Monk Hood's store.'

'Don't tell me – he's a gangster, too,' said Garth, pulling a face.

'He's retired,' blurted Mickey idiotically.

'What's that supposed to mean?' asked Garth. He was beginning to wonder if the street kid was trying to set them up. Perhaps the best thing to do was to get rid of him.

Violet was thinking something completely different. It was clear to her that Madame Poisson didn't know what they were talking about. She must have been up on one of her dawn walks and had not heard the gossip or seen a newspaper. Violet knew that if she found out she would never let them anywhere near the Bowery. Yet if they went, there might be a slim chance that they could find out more about Paul Kelly. Violet looked sideways at Mickey. Perhaps he could be persuaded to help them.

Further down the street, she saw a flower girl holding out a tray of violets. Violets were Madame Poisson's favourite flowers and she had been searching for them since they had arrived. 'Look! Madame! Violets! We'll wait here for you!'

As Madame Poisson hurried away, Violet turned back to Mickey. 'What do you know about Paul Kelly?'

'Nuffin'.'

'Is your friend Monk Hood a gangster, too?' demanded Violet. She knew she probably sounded ridiculous but, then again, what was there to lose?

Now it was Mickey who wished he'd run off and left these strange people on their own. There was no way he wanted this girl asking silly questions in the Bowery. It wasn't worth the dollar the fish-faced lady had given him for grabbing the monkey.

'I told you,' muttered Mickey. 'Monk Hood's retired. Keeps a pet store now.'

Violet was so excited she wasn't listening. The idea of going to a retired gangster's pet store thrilled her and more than ever she was determined to find out anything she could about Paul Kelly. Even if it meant stopping strangers on the street.

Meanwhile Garth was beginning to come round to her way of thinking. His voice broke into her thoughts. 'Are you going to stand there like a dumb donkey all day or do we catch a tram to the Bowery?' He turned to Mickey and spoke fast in a low voice. 'There's five bucks for you if you don't run off.'

Mickey stared into Garth's face. He wasn't as stupid as this well-dressed young man thought. 'I ain't goin' nowhere.'

SIX

Monk Hood gave Violet a puzzled look. He'd never met an English lady before, let alone one in fancy clothes with a funny accent. All she'd done since she walked into his shop was to ask questions. Now she wanted to know why he had chosen to call his store Pigeon Palace.

Monk scratched his unshaven jowls. 'I likes de boids, Miss. Deys allays been friends to me.' Monk's face clouded over and his flat ears seemed to flatten even more against his bullet head. 'Any guy gets gay wi' a boid in my neck of woods, I beat him up, see?'

'Yes, of course,' said Violet slowly. She looked at

the brass knuckle dusters on the man's thick stubby fingers. 'I do see.'

'*Violette*,' interrupted Madame Poisson, who to Garth's discomfort seemed to have taken to retired gangsters as well as street urchins. 'You must stop pestering Monsieur 'Ood with your questions.' She turned and beamed at him. 'We are 'ere to buy a cage. Which cage would you suggest, Monsieur 'Ood?'

'Dere's all sorts out de back, lady,' said Monk Hood, staring at the bustling figure with his dull grey eyes. 'I'll show yus.'

Garth watched in amazement as Madame Poisson almost linked arms with the ex-gangster and followed him through the dirty store.

Garth stared around him. The room he was in was badly lit and smelled of stale straw and the rank smell of old bird droppings. Around the walls, a few lop-eared rabbits stared mindlessly through the bars in their cages. In a large glass aquarium, a green turtle sat on a flat stone in the middle of a puddle of stagnant water. It looked as if it hadn't moved for years. Different coloured dog collars and leather leads with gold metal clips dangled from the walls. Everything was covered in dust. It occurred to Garth that Monk Hood didn't have many customers.

He turned to where Mickey was staring at a single goldfish with unconvincing concentration. Ever since they had walked through the door, the street kid had looked uncomfortable and Garth wondered whether he was beginning to regret accepting the five dollars. It was clear that Mickey and Monk Hood knew each other very well indeed as Garth had suspected. Mickey probably owed the older man a favour, and no doubt he had hoped that Violet would buy a cage for twice its usual price and they would split the difference.

Suddenly, a canary began to sing from a dark corner of the room.

Mickey almost jumped out of his skin.

'Why are you so nervous?' asked Garth. He walked over to the goldfish bowl. 'Is there something about this place you forgot to mention?'

Mickey glared at Garth's suspicious face. 'Yus wanted to come 'ere. I needed the money,' he muttered. Once again, Mickey wanted to cut and run and if it hadn't been for the five dollars he would have shot out of the door that minute.

'So, where does Mook Hood fit in?' asked Garth sharply.

'I brought yus here in good faith,' said Mickey. 'Look, I owes the guy a favour. Please. Buy de munkey a cage and let's get out of 'ere.' Mickey looked around him. 'I hate dis place.'

Violet looked up from where she was kneeling beside a box of kittens. She had also sensed Mickey's edginess from the moment he walked into the shop. She decided to take him off-guard. 'What do you know about Paul Kelly?'

'Nuffin'!' Mickey almost shouted. 'And I don't want to, neither. He's a bad, bad man.' His mouth twisted in his face. 'I wish I'd never brought yus 'ere.'

'*Violette!*' Madame Poisson stood in the middle of the room, holding up a large gilt metal cage by a thin piece of string. 'Is this not exactly the right size?' She jerked the cage higher and the string snapped.

Clang! The cage hit the floor with a deafening crash. All the other cages in the room jangled as their terrified occupants ran about behind the bars. The only animal in the store who wasn't locked up was Homer. He leaped off Violet's back, swung himself up a small spiral staircase and disappeared through a skylight window.

'I'll get him this time,' yelled Garth. As he bounded up the stairs, he turned back to Violet. 'Just buy the cage, will you?'

There was something in his voice and something about the foul, dirty store that suddenly made Violet shiver. She nodded, white faced, and reached for her purse.

At the top of the stairs, a rickety door led onto the roof. Garth pulled it open and found himself in a small, flat area, surrounded by pigeon coops. All along the street, he could see other roofs with other coops and between the buildings, lines and lines of greyish scraps of laundry. As he stood for a moment, looking out at endless balconies, their broken railings hung with yet more clothes, he was aware of a pigeon fluttering onto the ledge. It walked stiff-legged towards a coop that sat apart from the others.

Garth watched, astonished, as Homer appeared from behind the coop and, with a quick flick of his skinny paw, seized the pigeon and carefully undid the shiny metal carrier tube attached to its ankle. A second later, the tube was heading towards his mouth.

'Don't eat it, Homer!' cried Garth, asking himself even as he spoke whether he was going mad. 'It's bad for you. Anyway I want to see what's inside it.'

The monkey looked up at him as if he was listening. He held the tube at arm's length, sniffed it once and scrambled up Garth's leg.

'Not so dumb, eh?' said Garth, as Homer pushed the tube into his fingers. The metal was warm from the monkey's paw. Garth was about to take a look at it when the stairs creaked and Mickey stood at the door.

'Holy rollers,' he said, looking about him. 'The Monk keeps carrier pigeons.'

'You didn't know?' said Garth.

Mickey shook his head slowly. Now, more than ever, he wanted to get out of the store.

Garth stared at Mickey's ashen face. 'What's so strange about keeping carrier pigeons?'

'Nuffin',' said Mickey, quickly. 'Absolutely nuffin'.' He took a piece of string and handed it to Garth. 'For Chrissake, tie up dat munkey and let's get out of here.'

Garth felt the message tube in his hand. And, as Mickey turned towards the door, he slipped it into his pocket.

SEVEN

'Who would have thought the codfish would be so soft?' said Garth, as he and Violet climbed quickly up the stairs to their day room at the top of the house. 'She was almost spoon-feeding him.'

Violet laughed. 'I'd say the housekeeper here had something to do with it. Mrs Murphy's Irish and they stick together.'

'But he's a street kid,' replied Garth. 'He'll strip the place given half a chance.'

Violet stopped on the stairs. 'I think that's a bit unfair. He *did* rescue Homer for me.'

'We paid him.'

'So what? He earned it.' Violet thought of the

scene they had just left in the kitchen. There had been Mickey, flanked on either side by two middle-aged women, clucking around him like mother hens. She smiled to herself. She would never forget the look on Mickey's grimy face. He couldn't believe his luck. He had clearly expected to be thrown back onto the streets. 'Besides, he's done us a favour,' said Violet. She paused. 'I had a hunch he might.'

'What do you mean?'

Violet threw Garth a sharp look. 'You'd never have found that message tube.'

Garth rolled his eyes. 'Come on, Vi. For all we know there's nothing in it.'

'But you said Mickey was surprised about the carrier pigeons.'

'You're right, he was.' Garth held out the small metal tube. 'Open it.'

Violet took the tube and began to unscrew it. 'Did Mickey see you had this?'

Garth shook his head.

'You don't trust him, do you?'

'No.' Garth looked into Violet's face and tried

to ignore the look of irritation he saw there. 'And you shouldn't either.'

Violet shrugged. 'He's the only person we've met who might be able to help us find Louis.'

'The police will find Louis—' Garth stopped. Violet's face had gone white. She was staring at the tiny piece of paper that was unrolled in her hand. 'What is it?'

'Read it,' said Violet in a voice barely above a whisper.

Garth took the piece of paper from her hand and held it up to the light. His heart thumped in his chest. On it were the words *Tell Kelly. Colbolt will cooperate.*

'Oh, my Lord!' said Garth slowly. He sat down on the edge of the sofa. 'This changes everything.'

Violet hurried towards the door. 'We've got to stop Mickey from leaving. We'll never find him again if he goes.'

At that moment, the door opened and Madame Poisson hurried into the room. '*Violette.* Garth. A Miss Daisy Van Horn is in the drawing room. She is very –' the French governess paused as if searching for the right word, '– anxious to see you.'

'Where's Mickey?' Violet asked urgently as if she hadn't heard what Madame Poisson had just said to her.

'Ah! Yes, that is the other news.' Madame Poisson beamed. 'Mrs Murphy has given Mickey a job. From tomorrow, he peels potatoes!'

'So he's coming back?' blurted Violet.

'Of course.' Mme Poisson looked back and forth between Garth and Violet. 'Is something the matter? Will Lady Eleanor say no, do you think?'

'Lady Eleanor never goes into the kitchen,' replied Violet.

A faint guilty blush spread over Madame Poisson's whiskery face. 'That is what Mrs Murphy said, too.' She smoothed her skirt to recover herself. 'Now, quickly, Garth. Run and fetch Miss Van Horn. You may receive her here if you would prefer. I will ask the maid to send up tea.'

'That's very kind of you, Madame,' said Violet. She hesitated. 'Will you join us?'

The little governess knew very well that Violet was only asking out of courtesy. 'Thank you,

Violette. But if you will excuse me, I must return to my sewing machine.'

Violet smiled. '*Another* shirtwaister, Madame?'

'Yes, indeed, *ma chère*,' replied Madame Poisson in a delighted voice as she turned to leave the room. 'This one is edged with blue ribbon!'

Ten minutes later, Violet was pouring out a cup of tea for Daisy Van Horn. She handed it over across the table. Daisy took it but her hand was shaking so much the tea slopped over the side into the saucer.

'I'm so sorry,' she whispered in a miserable voice, the teacup still wobbling in her hand. 'But I just didn't know what else to do.'

Garth leaned forward and put the cup carefully on the table. 'Tell us everything you can, Daisy,' he said quietly. 'We know Louis is in trouble and we want to help him, too.'

Daisy clenched her fingers together and stared down at her dress. 'I don't understand,' she wailed. 'Why hasn't Papa given Louis any money for the portrait? Why does he look so angry all the time?'

She burst into tears and buried her face in her hands. '*Where is Louis?*'

Garth looked over Daisy's heaving shoulders at Violet. He was hopeless when girls started to cry. He never knew what to do with them. He got up and walked to window.

Violet leaned forward and put her hand on Daisy's arm. 'Look, Daisy,' she said firmly. 'We're just as worried as you. But we can't help find Louis unless you tell us everything you know.'

'We're engaged,' whispered Daisy. She sniffed and rubbed her nose with a white lacy handkerchief. 'It's a secret. Not even Mama knows.'

She suddenly jerked up her head and stared at Violet with the startled eyes of a rabbit. 'You must promise not to tell anyone,' she cried. 'You see, I don't think Mama or Papa would approve.'

Garth returned from the window and sat down on the arm of the old leather chair. 'Of course we won't tell anyone. But with all respect, Daisy, that isn't going to help us find Louis.' He took a deep breath. 'What do you know about Paul Kelly?'

'I'd never seen him before,' said Daisy, so quickly

that both Violet and Garth knew she was lying. 'He's horrible.'

'We think your father knows him,' said Violet, gently. 'The moment he saw him at your reception, he looked so furious.' She paused. 'It almost looked as if they'd had some kind of falling out.'

'Papa would never know such a man,' insisted Daisy. 'He's a gangster! Mama said so!' She went bright red and clutched at her handkerchief. 'I mean, everyone says so.'

'We think Louis owed Paul Kelly money,' said Garth, slowly.

'How?' cried Daisy.

'We don't know how,' said Violet. 'But Louis was obviously frightened of him.' She paused again. 'And so were you. I watched you both, very carefully. Are you sure you haven't met him before?'

'I never *met* him!' Daisy almost shouted.

'But you've *seen* him,' said Garth.

'Yes!' cried Daisy, desperately. 'Yes! I've *seen* him.' She burst into tears all over again. 'I saw him with my father!'

Violet pulled the bell cord for more tea. Then

she and Garth listened as Daisy told them what had happened that February day on the way to Brooklyn Bridge.

The next time Violet poured out tea, Daisy held her cup without spilling it. 'I love Louis,' she said quietly. 'I believe I love him more than Mama and Papa.' As she spoke she pulled a ribbon from around her neck and held out a locket in the palm of her hand. 'I'll do anything to help find him.'

Violet stared at the locket. 'Is there a picture inside?'

Daisy opened the locket. Inside was a miniature of Louis. 'He painted it himself.'

Violet stared at Louis Colbolt's huge dark eyes and pale, high cheekbones. 'Would you lend us this, Daisy?' she asked. She looked up into Daisy's tear-stained face. 'We would have a much better chance of finding Louis if we could show someone what he looked like.'

It didn't even occur to Daisy to ask who that someone might be, but Garth knew Violet was thinking of Mickey.

Daisy swallowed a great sob. 'You won't lose it, will you?' she pleaded. 'It's all I have left.'

After supper that evening, Madame Poisson went back to her sewing machine and Garth and Violet were on their own once more. Which was exactly what they had hoped for. Lord Percy and Lady Eleanor had left earlier to go to the opera and then on to a gala dinner at the Waldorf Astoria. Violet had kissed her mother goodbye with relief. They wouldn't be back until late, which meant her mother would not leave her bedroom until noon the next day. So Garth and Violet could be out and away before she had time to ask awkward questions or, even worse, insist that Violet come shopping with her again.

Garth put down the metal message tube on the table between them. 'What do you think?'

Violet straightened out the fingers of both hands as if she was trying to straighten out her thoughts. 'I think . . .' she said slowly, 'I think Paul Kelly is keeping Louis prisoner somewhere.' She looked at the tiny, curled-up message. 'What was it you heard him say after the reception?'

'"All I need is a little help with a camel-hair brush."' Garth looked up at Violet. 'What's that supposed to mean?'

'Maybe he wants a painting faked.' Violet thought of the rows of brushes in her watercolour box. 'Camel-hair brushes can be very fine.'

'If Louis is useful to Kelly then we know he's safe.' Garth thought of the desperation he had heard in Louis' voice. 'If we could only find out what hold Kelly has on him. Apart from stealing his portrait.'

'It *must* be gambling debts.' Violet ran her fingers through her thick curly hair. 'But we need to find out how Daisy Horn's father comes into it. I'm sure now they're all connected.'

'So am I. And the only person who can help us is Mickey. He knows the Bowery like the back of his hand.'

Violet stood up and looked out over Washington Square. Chandeliers twinkled in the huge windows of the houses opposite. The *clip clop* of horses' hooves floated up through the air. 'I'll talk to the codfish. She'll have to ask Mrs Murphy if we can have Mickey to ourselves for a bit.' She paused. 'I'm sure he'll see things our way.'

'I hope so. But he was pretty frightened when Paul Kelly's name came up last time.' Garth picked up the message tube and put it carefully in his pocket. 'I'm tired, Vi,' he muttered. 'I'll feel better tomorrow.'

'It's because Louis is your friend, too,' said Violet gently. 'Don't worry. We'll find him. And we'll stop this bad business, *whatever* it is.'

'Top o' the morning, Miss Violet! Master Garth! Mrs Murphy says you've work for me.'

Violet and Garth were sitting on their favourite bench, hidden behind the hedge at the bottom of the garden.

Now Violet stared at Mickey in astonishment. The boy who stood in front of them looked completely different from the one they had last seen in the kitchen the day before. He wore a pair of brown wool trousers and a checked flannel shirt. His face was scrubbed and shiny and even the boots on his feet looked half polished. Then Violet remembered that Mrs Murphy had mentioned a set of clothes she had bought for her grandson for St Patrick's Day. But unexpectedly her son had got a job in a meat-packing plant and the whole family had moved to Chicago.

Violet smiled to herself. No wonder Mrs Murphy had taken to the urchin Madame Poisson had brought in off the streets. Mickey and her grandson must be about the same age.

'Did no one tell yus it's rude to stare?' Mickey asked Violet in a teasing voice. 'Yer eyes get stuck, did ya know that?' He produced a bag of cookies from behind his back. 'Peanut-butter cookies. Mrs Murphy's compliments.'

There were crumbs down the front of Mickey's shirt.

'Tasty enough for you?' asked Garth.

'Delicious, thanks,' replied Mickey without batting an eyelid.

Violet took a cookie and nibbled at it thoughtfully. She had already spoken to Madame Poisson to ask if Mrs Murphy would allow Mickey to come with them on their trips around the city. *He'll be able to tell us so many things we could never find out ourselves, Madame.*

It was a long shot but to Violet's delight, her dear codfish agreed completely. Madame Poisson had a great curiosity for all things American and Mickey had already filled her head with stories. The day they had come back from the pet store Mickey had pointed out the fancy restaurants on Broadway called lobster palaces. *'They's gold inside, see? Floor, ceiling, tables, chairs — jus' like a king's palace. An' the fancy folk, they eats nothing but lobster dinners.'*

A look of pure delight had spread over Madame Poisson's face and Violet saw her mouth form the words *lobster palace* almost as if she was tasting the meat itself.

Now the moment had come to find out if Mickey would help them track down Louis. Watching Mickey's face closely, Violet handed him the locket.

Immediately she saw a flicker of recognition in Mickey's eyes. Then, just as quickly, he changed his expression and stared down at the locket as if he was looking at a sparkly stone he'd found on the beach.

'He's a painter called Louis Colbolt,' said Garth, trying to keep his voice even. 'He's a friend of mine and the thing is, he's gone missing, and we're desperate to find him.'

Violet was expecting Mickey to suggest they ask the cops but instead he looked more closely at the picture. 'Did he paint this himself?'

Garth nodded. 'It's called a miniature.' He paused. 'Because it's small.'

'So what else does 'e paint?' asked Mickey, handing back the locket. 'My gran had a painting of a buncha flowers, once. Does he paint flowers?'

It was clear to Violet that Mickey was trying to distract them. 'Portraits, mainly,' she said. 'Louis's good at getting likenesses.'

Mickey stared at her. 'Wha' does that mean?'

'It means he can make things look like what they are.' Garth paused. 'People or things.'

'So he could copy bank notes?' blurted Mickey.

At that moment, Madame Poisson bustled up from behind the hedge.

'What is this talk of copying bank notes, Mickey?' she asked, straightening his collar affectionately. She waggled a finger at Garth and Violet. 'Really, you two, you must *'elp* Mickey with his language.'

Madame Poisson turned back to Mickey. 'You don't *copy* bank notes, young man. You *forge* them.' And she bustled away before she could see the colour drain from Mickey's face.

For a split second, Garth, Violet and Mickey were frozen to the spot. Then just as Mickey turned to run, Garth grabbed him by the shoulder and shoved him forcefully down on the bench.

'Cut out the innocent act, you little street rat,' he snarled. 'You're hiding something from us.'

Violet had never seen Garth so angry. The last thing she wanted was a fight to break out between them. 'Look, Mickey,' she said. 'I know you've seen Louis before. I saw it in your face when I showed you his picture.'

'I ain't seen no one,' muttered Mickey, still squirming under Garth's hold. 'Let go of my shoulder. You're hurting me.'

'Louis is hurting more with every lie you tell,' said

Garth furiously. He tightened his grip. 'Now tell me what you know.' He put his face an inch away from Mickey's. 'Or I'll make good and sure Mrs Murphy throws you back out onto the street.'

Mickey's face crumpled. 'Don't do that! Please, don't do that!' His eyes filled. 'These are the first decent clothes I've ever had!'

'Then tell us what you know,' repeated Violet calmly.

Mickey sniffed and wiped his nose with the back of his sleeve. 'Oirright. Oirright. I did see yer man.'

'When?' asked Garth.

'In the Bowery, couple of nights ago. I noticed him 'cos of his clothes. You don't get fancy clothes like that down there.' He stared uncomfortably at his feet. 'Anyway, they seemed fancy to me.'

Garth looked across at Violet. 'It must have been the same night as the reception. Paul Kelly must have taken him there after you saw him get into the cab.'

At the mention of Paul Kelly's name, Mickey jumped up from the bench. 'No one said nuffin' about Paul Kelly. I ain't 'avin nuffin' to do wiv 'im!'

Suddenly Garth heard Louis' voice in his head. *'You're a crook! If I do what you want I'll be a crook, too!'* 'That's it!' he shouted. *'That's* what the camel-hair brush is about.'

Garth stared at Violet and his face was red and excited. 'Paul Kelly's running some counterfeit scam and he's making Louis work for him.' He turned to Mickey. 'And you know something about it, don't you? You just asked if he copied bank notes.'

Mickey shook his head and said nothing. It was one of the stupidest questions he had ever asked in his life.

Garth pulled out the metal message tube and shoved it in Mickey's face. 'Guess where I found this?'

'Wrapped round a pigeon's leg,' said Mickey. 'So what?'

'I found it on the roof at Monk Hood's pet store.' Garth tightened his grip on Mickey's shoulder. 'Where *you* took us!' As he spoke Garth could feel himself getting angrier and angrier. Suddenly he realised that nothing had been a coincidence.

Mickey had followed them the day Homer escaped and if Homer hadn't escaped, Mickey would have stolen him anyway to get them to the Bowery.

'You took us there on purpose, you piece of garbage,' he hissed. 'What were you planning? To rob us? What else are you hiding?'

'It wasn't on purpose,' wailed Mickey. 'It was just as I told you. I owed Monk a favour. I caught de munkey and I thought I could pay him back.'

'What kind of favour?' snarled Garth.

Mickey slumped in his seat. 'He paid for my gran's coffin.'

'Oh, no!' said Violet under her breath.

Garth loosened his grip. 'If you're lying—'

'I'm not lying!' cried Mickey, wiping furiously at his cheeks. 'Look! I'll tell you straight. *Everything*. Just promise you won't send me back onto the streets.'

EIGHT

'Are you sure this is a good idea?'

Violet chewed her lips and looked uncomfortably at Garth. If she hadn't known him like a brother, she wouldn't have recognised him. Mickey had done a good job. The clothes Garth wore were barely more than rags. His heavy, oversized boots were tied up with twine. His face was smeared with soot and Mickey had rubbed a tiny bit of Madame's rouge at the edge of Garth's mouth so it looked as if he had been in a fight. One of his front teeth had been blackened and his fingernails were filthy and broken where he had dragged them through the mud at the bottom of the garden.

If it wasn't for the bright excitement in his eyes, Garth would have looked down and out and desperate.

'What happens if something goes wrong?' whispered Violet. Although they had gone over and over the plan with Mickey the night before, she was still frightened.

The plan had sounded simple enough. Mickey would take Garth to the Bowery and see what they could find out about Paul Kelly's counterfeiting scam and hopefully where he was keeping Louis.

During their conversation on the bench, Mickey had told Violet and Garth that the only thing he knew for sure about Paul Kelly was that he kept in touch with his gang members by carrier pigeon and it wasn't until he'd gone up onto the roof of Monk Hood's store that he'd realised that the gangster might not have retired after all. Mickey had also heard that Paul Kelly was making fake bills. He didn't know much about the way such scams worked but he did know that big bosses like Paul Kelly never got caught. It was the mugs who handled the fakes or made them that ended up taking the rap.

Mickey swore to them again and again that he hadn't known Monk Hood still had anything to do with Kelly. *'I tought he'd retired. Honest, you gotta believe me.'* And in the end, they did. There was something in his voice that was raw, as if he had nothing left to hide. And after all, as Garth had pointed out to Violet when Mickey was back in the kitchen with Mrs Murphy, 'He needs us as much as we need him, now.'

Violet had agreed, but trusting Mickey with Garth's safety was another matter entirely.

'I've got to see for myself, Vi,' Garth insisted.

'But you don't know the Bowery,' Violet said. 'And what happens if someone spots you hanging about with Mickey in one of Kelly's bars? They're not going to send you home in a cab, are they? And your eyes are wrong. They should be dull and empty like those people we saw on the street down there. You look like the cat who's eaten the cream and wants the caviar.'

'I'll watch my back,' Garth said gruffly. 'We've

got to find Louis before the counterfeit money goes on the street.'

Violet knew he was right and, in the end, she agreed to the plan. They decided that Violet would go with Madame Poisson to look at Brooklyn Bridge just as Daisy had done and would then insist on visiting the City Museum to see its collection of cowboy artefacts. Madame Poisson adored America's Wild West history so Violet knew it wouldn't be too difficult to persuade her. That would leave Garth and Mickey at least six hours to find out what they could in the Bowery's seedy bars and hotels. If Garth wasn't back in time for dinner, Violet would tell her father what they had done and the police would be called. There was no other choice.

Garth took one more look at his grimy reflection and grinned a gap-toothed grin. 'Maybe I'll test out my disguise on Mrs Murphy!'

Five minutes later, Violet watched from her window as Mrs Murphy shooed the street boy out of the garden, threatening to set the dogs on him. She took out the scarab pendant she had found in Egypt and squeezed it hard for good luck. Garth was going to need all the help he could get.

Now that he was on his own with Mickey, Garth felt much less confident and the Bowery seemed dirtier and nastier than he remembered. They walked quickly down the filthy streets, over-shadowed by huge tenement buildings on either side. The beaten mud alleys were crowded with men, women and children wrapped in rags, their pinched, pale faces telling anyone who cared to look that they were hungry and worn-out. Garth knew that sometimes more than fifty families lived in the rat-infested blocks that loomed above him and some of them were in rooms that didn't even have windows to let in fresh air. He shuddered. What kind of man was Paul Kelly that he could take money from such desperate people?

'OK,' said Mickey. He stopped and pointed to a shabby hotel in front of them, a drooping line of electric light bulbs hanging from its first-floor balcony. 'That's the Silver Dollar. It's one of Kelly's places an' we might as well start there.' He fixed

Garth with sharp eyes. 'Now, keep yer head down and don't get noticed.'

Garth nodded. His stomach was crawling with fear and he was beginning to wish he had listened when Violet had warned him of the danger he was putting himself in. She had been right. If something went wrong, no one would help him here. More likely, they'd bump him on the head and throw him in the river.

'Oi!' said Mickey, jabbing Garth in the ribs. 'You ain't listenin'! What did I jus tell yus?'

Garth shook his head numbly. 'Sorry, Mickey I . . .'

'Ya gotta listen, Garth. And whatever you do, say nuffin' when yer inside. That fancy voice o' yours'll give us both away.'

Garth looked around him, praying that · by the end of the afternoon he'd be back in Washington Square. Then he nodded nervously and followed Mickey round the hotel to the back entrance. There were piles of broken bottles and rotten food everywhere. As they edged up to the door, a rat the size of a small cat rushed in front of them. Garth had to pinch himself not to cry out.

'We can't go in the front,' explained Mickey quickly. 'They'd have us for pickpockets. OK, follow me.' He grinned. 'And remember I move fast.'

Five minutes later, Garth and Mickey were sitting in the corner of a low, smoky room full of men in cheap suits and women in gaudy, shiny dresses edged with floppy lace. The dresses looked as tired and worn as their owners. Garth knew they were the sort of clothes Mrs Murphy would have called 'plain nasty'. As for Lady Eleanor, Garth doubted she had ever seen such women in her life.

Around him, Garth saw a long polished wooden bar with a brass rail stretching the length of one wall. Rickety tables on the cracked plank floor were covered with glasses. At one end of the room, a girl with scarlet lips and rouged cheeks was singing a song about green hills and grandmothers' smiles. She sounded Irish. A wizened man wearing a crumpled felt hat tinkled on the keys of an upright piano beside her, a glass of whisky balanced on the bench beside him. Everyone's faces looked twisted and droopy as if they were made of melting wax.

'Good,' whispered Mickey in Garth's ear. 'They're all drunk. No one will notice us in this crowd. Now, this is what ya do. Pick up the empty glasses from the tables an' take them to the bar. Do it slowly and keep yer ears open.' Then he was gone.

Garth stood up and his knees turned to jelly. He watched as Mickey shuffled around a group of tables, picking up glasses and holding out his hand for a tip. Garth looked at his own hands. They were still too clean. He quickly rubbed them on the seat of his pants and again on the filthy floor. Then, with his heart banging, he got up and went over to the nearest table.

Three hours later, after listening to endless talk of vendettas against cops, plans to get rich quick, and bets on lucky horses, Garth finally heard the name he was hoping for. He had just put down some glasses at the bar when a fat man at a table in the corner leaned forward and spoke quickly but clearly to his companion. 'A little boid tells me Kelly's got a counterfeiting scam going.'

The other man leaned back in his chair. He was wearing a brown woollen coat with greasy velvet lapels and he was thin with a face like a ferret. 'Maybe,' he replied carefully.

'Dunno how 'e managed it,' said the fat man. 'Pinky O'Hara's just got ten years for painting pretty pictures on bank notes.' He rolled his whisky around his mouth. 'No one's as good as Pinky.'

The other man shrugged. 'Maybe 'e's found another Pinky.'

'Nah,' said the fat man. 'Pinky was the best.'

The ferret-faced man smiled knowingly. 'Maybe someone else is learning fast.' He swallowed his own drink and looked hard at his companion. 'I hear Kelly's found a painter.'

Garth felt his eyes bulge in his face and his heart began to hammer. He shoved the glasses along the bar to look as if he was busy.

'Nah,' said the fat man again. 'What would a painter be doing with the likes of Paul Kelly?'

The man in the brown coat pushed his glass forward. 'Trying to get back something he wants.' He smiled a nasty smile and showed a rotten front tooth. 'Kelly's got some portrait of his. They say yer man will do anything to get it back.'

'Like painting pictures on blank bank notes with a camel-hair brush?' asked the fat man.

'How should I know?' The other man stood up. 'Anyone ever tell you not to ask so many questions?'

'Nah,' said the fat man. He held up his glass for another drink. 'Why should they? I know all the answers.' Suddenly his face went hard. 'Anyone ever tell you, you talk too much?'

Garth saw fear flicker across the thin man's face as he turned and pushed his way quickly through the crowded room.

'What's yer hurry?' muttered a red-faced drunk. He stuck out his foot and the man in the brown coat fell flat on his face, knocking over a table of glasses as he went down.

No one seemed to notice the *smash* as the glasses hit the floor. It must have happened all the time. That is to say, no one except Garth and a man who walked into the bar at the same moment. Garth looked up and saw the glint of a gold-topped cane. The next second he found himself staring straight into the narrowed, yellow eyes of Paul Kelly.

113

Garth thought he was going to be sick. Even though he wanted to run, he couldn't move. He watched as Kelly turned to a henchman at his side and pointed at him.

'Jaysus! Ya great booby. *Get out of here!*' Mickey appeared at his elbow and began to pull him away.

When Garth still didn't move, Mickey shoved him in the small of the back and dragged him out of the bar, through the back corridor and out into the filthy back yard.

Behind them came the sound of angry voices.

'They're after us,' cried Mickey. He pulled Garth towards a rusty iron fire escape. 'Get up onto the roof. It's our only escape.'

Somewhere Garth found the strength to follow Mickey up the rickety stairs. With each step, Garth was sure the stairs would fall away from the crumbling brick wall.

Just as they reached the top, one of Paul Kelly's men jumped on the bottom rung.

'Kick the wall brackets,' cried Mickey. 'They're rusty. They'll break.'

For the first time, Garth was thankful for the

heavy, over-sized boots he was wearing. He kicked as hard as he could. Sure enough, the top of the stairs came away and tumbled down the side of the brick wall.

'Come on,' cried Mickey. 'They'll be waiting for us on the other side!' As they ran over the roof, dodging in and out of lines of wet clothes and piles of storage boxes, there was a howl of fury behind them. Mickey turned as if he was trying to make up his mind what to do next. Then he dodged to one side, bent double and went back on his tracks. Without any warning, he flung himself over the side of the roof and pulled Garth with him.

For a split second, Garth thought they were going to die – then they landed on a shallow platform four feet below.

Mickey turned to him and grinned. 'Short cut, see. They'll think we went the other way.'

Garth nodded dumbly.

'Dun' worry,' said Mickey. 'I'll get you back safe.' He looked at Garth's grey face and touched his arm. 'See, you can trust me.'

Garth managed a weak smile and set off beside him.

'So do you think we can trust him now?' asked Violet, after Madame Poisson had retired to her sewing machine on the strict understanding that they would both be reading the first two chapters of *The Rise and Fall of the Roman Empire* for discussion the next day.

She pushed aside the heavy history book and put her feet up on the low stool in front of her.

Garth nodded. After a shower and a big helping of Mrs Murphy's chicken cobbler, he was feeling a lot better. 'He could have left me there, Vi. Paul Kelly didn't see Mickey until he came to get me out.' He looked up. 'I'd have had it without him. I couldn't move.'

'So where is Mickey now?'

Garth shrugged. 'He ate something and left.' Garth paused and rubbed his hands over his face. 'Thing is, he can't go back to the Bowery now. We've got to look after him.'

Violet nodded. She had already worked that out

for herself. But a job peeling potatoes was not enough to keep Mickey in Washington Square if he decided to leave them and try his luck in another part of the city.

'I've spoken to Mrs Murphy,' said Violet. 'She'll give Mickey a proper job.'

Garth thought of Paul Kelly's gold-topped cane and his narrowed, tiger eyes. He shivered despite himself. 'It's only fair. We got Mickey into this in the first place.'

'Exactly. And what's more, when he comes back I think we should tell him everything.' Violet paused. 'Mickey will have a better idea how these people *think*.'

'You're right,' muttered Garth. 'I still can't work out how Philip Van Horn fits into this but I'm sure Mickey will. I mean, why would he ask Louis to paint Daisy's portrait, then not pay him?'

'Easy,' said Mickey from the doorway.

Violet nearly jumped out of her skin. 'How long have you been standing there?'

Mickey grinned. 'Long enough to know we can do business together.'

Violet didn't know whether to be furious or impressed. 'How did you manage to get up here without anyone seeing you?' she demanded. 'We didn't even hear you open the door.'

'That's because you weren't listening.' Mickey walked across the floor, light-footed as a fox. 'Mind if I sit down?'

'Of course not,' said Violet. Suddenly a smile spread across her face. The moment Mickey walked into the room, the atmosphere had changed. For the first time, she felt they might have a chance to find out some answers. 'So, Mr Smarty Pants, why didn't Van Horn pay Louis? And how does that connect him with Kelly?'

'Questions, questions!' Mickey's voice was teasing but his bright eyes were serious. 'OK. Look at it dis way. The reason Van Horn didn't pay Louis was to make 'im desperate.' Mickey paused. 'That's the easy bit.'

Garth sat up. He, too, had felt the change. 'And it worked, of course. He had gambling debts then he found out his mother was ill. But where does Kelly come in?'

'I was getting to dat,' replied Mickey. 'See, it wouldn't matter to Van Horn whether he paid Louis double what they agreed. He's got more money than a Wall Street bank. The point is that it must 'ave been *Kelly* who wanted *Louis* to be really desperate so he leant on Van Horn. So that means Kelly's got someting on Van Horn otherwise Van Horn would 'ave never agreed.'

Violet remembered the fury on Philip Van Horn's face when he had seen Kelly at the reception. Then she thought of Daisy's description of her father's expression after she had seen him leaving Kelly in the Bowery in February. It was just as she had thought: there had been a falling out. An agreement must have been made and broken. 'It has to be something pretty big,' she said.

Garth was thinking the same thing. He quickly told Mickey what Daisy had seen from her cab window and then what had happened at the reception.

Mickey raised his eyebrows. 'So maybe Kelly's blackmailing him.'

'It would fit, certainly.'

'Which means that Mr Philip Van Horn isn't the pillar of Society that he makes out to be,' said Violet slowly. She turned to Garth. 'We didn't find a hint of anything suspicious when we looked him up in the library.'

'The big guys cover their tracks,' said Mickey. 'An' if Van Horn was tied up with Paul Kelly in any way, it's gotta 'ave been something real bad. That man's the devil.' Mickey's face went serious. 'We gotta find your friend fast.'

'What do you mean?' asked Violet.

'Kelly don't bother with people he don't need no more,' replied Mickey in a matter-of-fact voice. 'And he don't keep promises neither. When Louis finishes the job, he could just disappear.'

'What do you mean?' asked Garth.

Mickey let out a deep breath. 'He could find himself in the river with a lump of cement tied to his foot. Nobody would ever find him.'

Violet's hand flew to her mouth and her face went the colour of wax. 'Oh, my God!'

Garth felt a coldness pass through him. His father had disappeared into thin air. Could it be possible that his father, as a lawyer, had somehow crossed Kelly? From what he had read in the old newspaper cuttings, everyone knew Kelly was a criminal but the police couldn't get anyone to give evidence against him so no lawyer could take him to court. But could his father have tried? It was impossible to find out. Garth hadn't been able to find a single sentence to connect his father with Kelly. Mickey was right. The big guys knew how to cover their tracks.

Suddenly a great anger surged through Garth and he felt his face harden. 'This time, Kelly isn't going to get away with it,' he said so fiercely that Violet was taken aback.

'Are you with us?' Garth turned to Mickey and held out his hand.

Mickey shook Garth's hand. Then Violet offered hers. 'I'm with yus.'

At that moment, the door opened and Madame Poisson came into the room. She didn't mention the obvious fact that neither Garth nor Violet were reading their history books or that Mickey was upstairs when he should have been in the servants' quarters.

'Ah! Mickey! There you are, you little scamp! Mrs Murphy wants to speak to you.' She paused and gave him a mysterious look. '*Mam'selle Violette's* particular instructions!'

Mickey's face fell and his eyes suddenly flicked suspiciously between Violet and Garth. 'You ain't double crossed me, 'ave ya?'

Violet blushed scarlet. 'I'm sorry, Mickey,' she said quickly. 'I thought you had overheard when you were standing in the doorway.'

Mickey watched her through hard eyes. 'Overheard what?'

'Mickey,' said Violet gently. 'Mrs Murphy wants to offer you a permanent job in the house. A dollar a day, all you can eat and your own bed.'

Madame Poisson stood with her hands on her hips and beamed. 'You will be a proper kitchen boy, not just a potato-peeler boy and I shall teach you myself 'ow to slice carrots and onions the *French* way!'

Mickey stared and said nothing. His mouth moved up and down but no words came out.

'You will accept, won't you?' pleaded Violet. 'You see, we were worried—'

Garth flashed her a look of warning and Violet stopped speaking.

'*You* were worried!' cried Madame Poisson. 'Mrs Murphy and myself were upset extremely! A young boy on the streets with no one to look after 'im!' She touched Mickey's arm. 'Your poor dear auntie!'

Violet went from scarlet to a hot purple. In order to be sure she got Mrs Murphy on her side, she had told her that Mickey's last relation had died and now there was no one to look after him. She looked uncomfortably at Mickey. 'I told Mrs Murphy about your aunt dying and . . .'

It took Mickey a split second to work out what Violet had done and why. Everything about him changed. 'That was good of you, Miss Violet,' he replied in a suitably subdued voice. He looked up at Madame Poisson. 'Poor dear Auntie Joan, the nearest ting I had to a family. God rest 'er soul.'

Madame Poisson wiped her eyes and blew her nose with a piece of patterned cloth she held in her hand. 'You will accept our offer, won't you, *mon petit*?'

'Accept?' cried Mickey. He held out his hand and

Madame Poisson took it in both of hers. 'To me, 'tis more of a miracle than an offer, and I tank you from the bottom of my heart!'

That night, Violet couldn't sleep. She was worried sick about Louis and she kept running through what Mickey had said about Paul Kelly and Philip Van Horn. What had Van Horn done in the past that had allowed Kelly to blackmail him now? There *must* be a way to find out. She forced her mind back to when they had first arrived in New York and her mother had been talking about some of the people she and Garth would meet. One of them was certainly Philip Van Horn, since he had known Garth's father. Violet tried to recall what her mother had said about Philip Van Horn, apart from the fact that he had trained as an architect and emigrated from Holland. Violet knew that he had not been rich when he'd first arrived in America because her mother had said that he had married his wife for her money. Violet tossed and turned. Lady Eleanor was most definitely a snob but her instincts were always accurate. And she didn't like Philip Van Horn. He was too 'pushy', which Violet knew meant that he was too single-minded or even ruthless — not acceptable characteristics in the 'right sort'. Despite his wealth, even Violet could sense that Philip Van Horn would do whatever it took to get what he wanted.

Just like Paul Kelly.

Could it be possible that somehow the two men had been involved in some business together? It seemed incredible to believe that someone like Philip Van Horn could have dealings with a known gangster. But then perhaps Paul Kelly had been different when he was a young man, too.

Violet swung her legs out of bed and crossed over the carpeted floor to where her window looked over the back garden. There was a bright full moon and the shadows on the ground were hard and sharp.

So it was sheer chance she saw Mickey appear from behind a hedge, shin up the black, cast-iron railings and land like a cat onto the empty cobbled street below.

NINE

Lady Eleanor looked into her daughter's dark, serious blue eyes. It struck her for the first time that Violet was going to turn into a beautiful young woman, and she was pleased because she had not anticipated it.

'I beg your pardon, dear,' she murmured. 'My mind was quite elsewhere. What was it you said?'

Violet tried to hide her irritation. She had decided to have a serious conversation with her mother about Philip Van Horn and Lady Eleanor's attention was already wandering.

'Why don't you like him?'

Lady Eleanor shrugged elegantly and rearranged her embroidered shawl around her shoulders. 'It's not that I don't *like* him, my dear, I merely believe he would be happier in a cage.'

'*What?*'

'Violet!' cried her mother sharply. There was nothing like coarseness to sour Lady Eleanor's mood. 'How dare you speak like a trollop!'

Violet felt her cheeks go hot. Why was it that every time she tried to talk to her mother, things always went horribly wrong? 'I'm sorry, Mama,' she muttered. 'I didn't meant to be rude. I just don't understand why you think Mr Van Horn would be happier in a cage.'

'What on *earth* are you talking about?' replied Lady Eleanor, trying in vain to quell a rising tide of exasperation. She couldn't understand it. Why did Violet feel it necessary to talk such utter nonsense all the time? Did she think she was being clever? Lady Eleanor had been quite prepared to suggest they lunch together and perhaps afterwards visit a sweet little Hungarian dressmaker Mrs Stuyvesant Fish had told her about. But now she had changed her mind. It was such a pity. Especially when Mrs Stuyvesant Fish had been so very complimentary about Violet after they had unexpectedly met in the drawing room.

Violet tried to control the irritation that was making her heart hammer in her chest. 'We were talking about Mr Van Horn, Mama,' she said patiently. 'I believe you were thinking of Homer.'

Now it was Lady Eleanor's turn to be irritated because, of course, Violet was right. 'That ridiculous little animal,' she cried, twisting her emerald engagement ring round and round her slender finger. 'I should never have allowed you to bring him with you. He's caused nothing but trouble since he arrived here.'

'Mama!' cried Violet. 'If it hadn't been for Homer, we would never have met Mickey.'

Lady Eleanor drew her brows together. 'Who's Mickey?'

Instantly Violet wished the floor would open and swallow her up. She hadn't intended to say anything about Mickey. It was only that he had been on her mind ever since she'd seen him climb over the railings in the middle of the night. He must have been heading back to the Bowery to find out what he could about Louis.

'Mickey's the new kitchen boy,' said Violet miserably.

'The kitchen boy!' repeated Lady Eleanor disdainfully. 'What interest could you possibly have in the kitchen boy?'

None! screamed Violet in her mind. *None at all, except that he might find Louis before Paul Kelly ties a concrete block to his leg and throws him in the river!*

The door opened and Lord Percy walked into the room. He took one look at his wife and his daughter and told Violet that Garth was in the garden waiting for her. The fact he hadn't seen Garth that morning didn't matter to Lord Percy. What did matter was that it was very clear his daughter needed some fresh air.

Violet got up from her chair and, ignoring the fact that her mother barely acknowledged her, ran gratefully out of the room.

She came into the front hall just as Garth shot

down the banister and landed with a whoop of delight and a perfect forward somersault onto the black and white marble tiles that covered the floor.

Garth's obvious good mood infuriated Violet. She glared at her layers of skirts and petticoats and stamped her foot hard on the floor. 'It's not fair,' she shouted. 'What if *I* wanted to slide down the banisters?' She was so angry her voice was trembling.

'Violet!' Garth looked up, startled. 'What's wrong?'

'My mother!' replied Violet furiously. 'Sometimes I absolutely loathe her!'

'My mother's a monster.'

The voice was high and tinkling like something that might have come out of the painted rosebud mouth of a doll.

Violet spun around in utter confusion. Daisy Van Horn was standing in front of her. Beside her, Dottie the parlour maid was purple with embarrassment.

''Scuse me, Miss,' she said. 'I did announce Miss Van Horn. I thought as you'd heard me.'

'Don't worry, Dottie,' said Violet. She felt her

cheeks go hot again. 'I was probably making too much noise to hear you.'

'Thank you, Miss.' Dottie bobbed and hurried away as fast as she could.

Violet steeled herself to look at Daisy. 'I'm sorry,' she said slowly. 'I don't usually speak of my mother in such disrespectful terms.'

There was a new, hard look in Daisy's eyes. 'Please don't apologise. Your mother was kind to Louis. I watched her introduce him to those rich old dinosaurs.' Daisy paused and took a breath. 'My mother, however, is a monster.'

Now it was Garth's turn to look away. He couldn't believe Daisy Van Horn would ever say such a thing. The *tick tock* of the grandfather clock echoed around the hall. At the other end of the corridor, behind the sitting-room door, Violet could hear her father's low voice and her mother's higher pitched interjections. A servants' bell rang below them and muffled footsteps sounded on the kitchen stairs.

'Let's go outside,' said Garth quickly. He led the way through the French doors into the garden. Violet and Daisy followed quickly behind him.

131

They all sat down on the bench overlooking the street and nobody knew what to say.

'How are you, Daisy?' asked Violet at last, even though it was perfectly obvious that Daisy was in a terrible state.

'Dreadful,' said Daisy shortly. 'I came to ask you if you had any news of Louis.' She swallowed. 'And to tell you that my father has been acting very strangely lately.'

Garth exchanged looks with Violet. It was important to say nothing and let Daisy talk.

'I hope you don't think any less of me for speaking like this of my father,' said Daisy. 'But I understand now that my loyalty lies with Louis.' Her hands made two fists in her lap. 'And, increasingly, I am sure my father is involved in his disappearance.'

Violet could barely hide the astonishment on her face.

'In what way is your father acting strangely?' asked Garth smoothly.

'He sleeps in his study, and at night he stays up drinking and talking to himself. One time I looked through the keyhole and I saw him pulling letters out of his desk and throwing them onto the fire.' Daisy shuddered. 'It felt like he was destroying evidence.'

Now it was Garth's jaw that dropped.

'And your mother?' asked Violet, quickly. 'Why did you call her, a, uh . . .'

'A monster?' said Daisy crisply. 'Because she is one. She screams at my father morning, noon and night. She says he has dragged her family's name into the mud and has ruined her life.'

'Why?' asked Violet.

'I don't know,' replied Daisy. 'But it all started after that horrible Paul Kelly turned up at the reception.' Suddenly Daisy's face crumpled and she burst into tears. 'I'm so worried about Louis! I'll kill myself if anything has happened to him. I'll throw myself off Brooklyn Bridge. I swear I will!'

Violet took a lace handkerchief from her pocket and handed it to Daisy, who sobbed and rubbed hard at her eyes. 'Have you heard anything about him?' she asked again. 'Do you know why he disappeared?'

Violet hesitated and looked at Garth. Garth nodded and Violet understood. They needed all the help they could get.

Half an hour later, Daisy Van Horn stood at the front gate and kissed Violet on the cheek. 'I'll do what I can,' she promised. 'But Father doesn't leave his study often.'

'Just look for anything that has Paul Kelly's name on it,' said Garth. 'It might be a note. It might be a newspaper clipping – but it will probably be at least twenty-five years old.'

Violet took Daisy's hand and held it. 'You must understand, Daisy, that we aren't accusing your father of having done anything wrong. All any of us know is that for some reason he is entangled with Paul Kelly. And that Louis is caught between them.'

Daisy Van Horn's doll eyes were as pale as the sky. 'My father has always done whatever was necessary to get what he wanted,' she said in a cold voice. 'Maybe for the first time in his life, he's regretting it.' She kissed Violet again and shook

Garth by the hand. Then without another word, she stepped up into the cab that was waiting for her in the square.

'Pssst!' A skinny arm was waving from the top of the outside stairs. 'I gotta talk to yus! What's that dame got to do with Paul Kelly?'

'Darn it, Mickey!' cried Garth. 'You can hear like a fox!'

Mickey vaulted over the top of the stairs towards them. 'When can we meet? I gotta tell ya some stuff.'

'What were you doing on the streets last night?' asked Violet.

'How'd you know that?' asked Mickey.

'I saw you from my window.'

'Yeah, well, I'd better be more careful next time, 'adn't I?'

'Michael Gallagher!' Mrs Murphy had a voice that sounded like a moose who'd swallowed a foghorn. 'Mr Edgar wants you in the pantry NOW!'

'We need a plan,' hissed Mickey. With one hand on the rail, he vaulted back again to swing himself down towards the kitchen. 'Word is Kelly's money's ready. As soon as it's on the streets, your friend's a dead man.'

'Do you know where they've got him?' asked Garth.

Mickey nodded and looked nervously over his shoulder. 'In a warehouse on Houston Street. The one overlooking the river.'

An outside door slammed at the bottom of the stairs. Mickey's face went white. Mrs Murphy was proving a tougher boss than he'd expected.

'We'll find you in the kitchen later,' cried Violet. By the time she had finished speaking, Mickey was already halfway down the steps.

At that moment, a cab rattled over the cobblestones and sent a flock of pigeons whirling into the sky. They circled above and flew away in different directions.

It was as if they each had a different place to go.

Violet clapped her hands, suddenly. 'Garth!' she cried. 'I think I know how we can help Louis escape!'

It was easy to persuade the codfish to go back to Monk Hood's pet store. Violet had slashed

Homer's old leash so he needed a new one, and any excuse to explore New York was good enough for Madame Poisson. The difficult bit was persuading Mrs Murphy to let Mickey have the afternoon off again. At last, Violet asked Madame to do the negotiations and, in return for a recipe for a *navarin* of lamb and a promise of sewing-machine lessons, the two women came to an agreement over their adopted street boy.

Mickey was delighted with the plan. While he was grateful for the clothes Mrs Murphy kept giving him, his new life as part of the family downstairs was beginning to feel a bit restrictive. Especially when the whiskery French woman began to correct his English grammar and teach him how to make his bed properly. The idea of gathering together some of his old street friends and returning to Monk Hood's store to get a few answers out of him made Mickey practically hop from foot to foot with delight.

Now he sat with Garth and Violet in the upstairs room, wriggling and kicking his feet while they waited for Madame Poisson to put the finishing touches to her new outfit.

'Remember, Mickey,' said Violet firmly. 'We don't want any horseplay from your friends. All they need to do is tie up Monk Hood and Garth will do the rest with a pair of scissors and a pigeon.'

'Can't I do that bit?' asked Mickey.

'No,' said Violet sharply. 'You cannot. Besides, maybe Monk Hood won't lie.'

''A course he'll lie.' Mickey looked at Garth. 'Pick up de pigeon and clip off its flying feathers. Dat'll change his mind.'

'Know something?' said Garth, smiling. 'I worked that out for myself.'

'Promise me you'll do exactly as you are told,' said Violet to Mickey. 'It's your job to distract Madame Poisson.'

'What happens if Monk pulls a knife on ya?' asked Mickey. He smirked. 'A pair o' pussies like you wouldn't know what was happenin'. I mean, *I'd* grab 'im by the wattles and whack 'im in the tombstones with me slipper!'

'Is that right?' said Garth patiently. 'So how would he able to tell us which pigeon came from Kelly's warehouse in Houston Street if you had already yanked his ears and knocked his teeth out?'

Mickey said nothing for a moment. 'I didn't tink of dat.'

'I thought not,' said Garth. 'See, we're not as stupid as you think. Don't forget, we only have one chance at this. If Kelly finds out, he'll move Louis somewhere else.'

Violet's face went serious. 'Or something worse.'

Mickey reached out and touched Violet's hand. 'Don' you worry, Miss Violet. I was only razzin' yus. Me and my friends'll be waiting round de pet store corner.'

Garth turned to Violet. 'Have you got the message ready?'

Violet nodded. She had searched all the paper shops in the neighbourhood for the same kind of scratchy cheap paper as the original message Garth had found. *Tell Kelly. Colbolt will cooperate.* At least two words were the same and Violet practised again and again so the handwriting looked identical. Now the message in the tube said, *Free Colbolt. Kelly's orders.* All Monk Hood had to do was give them the right homing pigeon.

*

An hour later, everything was going like clockwork. As soon as the cab stopped in front of Monk Hood's pet store and Madame Poisson stepped down onto the hard mud, a whistle from round the corner told Violet and Garth that Mickey and his friends were ready and waiting.

Violet and Garth stood in front of the grimy windows and peered inside. There was no sign of Monk Hood. 'Maybe he's closed,' said Madame Poisson, in a disappointed voice. She tried the door handle. It was locked.

'He's never closed,' called Mickey.

Madame Poisson, Garth and Violet looked up to see Mickey walking jauntily along the street with four boys his own age. Mickey stopped and introduced them. 'Dis redhead is Liam. De one with the scar is Dermot. Dis is Connor with the black eye and Job is de one whose mudder reads de Bible.' Job grinned and showed one missing front tooth. Mickey paused and looked sideways at Garth. 'Dey'd like their fifty cents up front if yus don't mind.'

'Give the boys their money, *cheri*,' cried Madame Poisson. 'It is, after all, so kind of them to help the *monsieur* clean out his cages.' The codfish wrinkled her nose and her eyes seemed to pop out even further. 'Poor *Monsieur* Monk 'as a bad back. 'E told me so himself.' She reached up to pull the doorbell but Mickey stopped her just in time. Now came the difficult bit and Violet and Garth had agreed that no one but Mickey could pull it off.

'Please, Ma'am, I 'as a favour to ask ya.'

Madame Poisson beamed down at Mickey's face, which had suddenly turned shy and hesitant. Watching him, Violet was sure he could be an actor one day. 'What favour is this, *mon petit?*'

'It's me Auntie Joan, de one that died. Her friend Mabel, de one that nursed her, well, she lives up de road. And she's right poorly herself.' Mickey turned to Violet, then fixed his big eyes back on Madame Poisson. 'Miss Violet here says you knows about medicines to make people better.' The big eyes filled with tears. 'She took bad this mornin', Ma'am. I swore on me auntie's grave, I'd bring you to see her.' He paused for a second to let his story sink in. 'Will ya come with me now, Ma'am? It won't take a moment, I swear.'

'But Mickey!' cried the little French governess in a flustered voice. She looked anxiously at Violet.

'I'll watch out for Violet,' said Garth firmly.

'I'm just going in to look at the kittens, Madame,' said Violet. 'And to choose another leash for Homer.'

'It'll only take a tiny while, Ma'am,' cried Mickey. He fixed pleading eyes on Madame Poisson's worried face. 'Please, fer Mabel's sake.' He pointed to a window in a building a little further along the road. 'She's only up there.'

Madame Poisson made her decision. 'Garth will be in charge,' she announced to the row of grinning faces. She didn't notice the sly twinkle in their eyes. 'You boys will do exactly what he says and *Violette*, you will confine yourself to the kitten box. We will ask *Monsieur* Monk which leash is best.'

Violet cast her eyes downwards as submissively as she could manage. '*Oui, Madame.*'

Mickey grabbed the little French governess's hand in case she changed her mind and began to pull her down the street. There was no time to lose.

Hairy Mary was a good actress but she had Donnegan's Bar to look after and, for a couple of dollars, she wasn't going to wait around all day.

TEN

Louis Colbolt pushed away a plate of fried chicken and buttered beets and stared hopelessly at his ink-stained fingers. He had never felt so miserable in all his life. At first, when Paul Kelly had driven him at speed through increasingly narrow streets to what seemed like the end of the world, he had convinced himself that he was doing the only thing possible to get himself out of the trouble he was in and to help his mother. So when he had been blindfolded and led up endless flights of stairs, he had determined to do the work Kelly wanted as quickly as he could, discharge his debts and reclaim his portrait.

But it had become clear the moment his blindfold

was removed that Paul Kelly had other ideas. Louis found himself in a large room with glass windows along one wall. Even at night, the lights of the city bathed the room in a murky yellow glow. He crossed to the window and peered through the glass. Below him was a river. To his right, Louis could see the steel cables of the Williamsburg suspension bridge, glimmering in the moonlight. He was east of the Bowery, maybe in Houston Street — if that was the ferry making its way through the black, choppy waters of the East River.

Behind him, Kelly switched on a light and everything became sickly green. Louis saw a long table covered in pots of ink, engraving pens and brushes. At one end was an enormous printing press. Beside it, blocks of evenly-cut paper were wrapped and stacked in tidy piles. Louis realised with a sinking heart that he was looking at a counterfeiting assembly line.

There was a *clank* of glass on bottle. Paul Kelly held out a tumbler of amber-coloured liquid. 'To lift your spirits, kid.'

Louis sniffed the liquor. It was bourbon. It was

what he always used to drink when he gambled. Suddenly his stomach turned over and he put the glass down on the table. 'No thanks,' he muttered. He was never going to drink bourbon again. 'So, what do you want me to do?'

Paul Kelly lit a cigar. 'Not me, kid. I'm no expert. The boys'll run you through the game tomorrow.' He smiled lazily and rested a hand on Louis' arm. 'All I need is your promise to cooperate. Then we'll both be happy.'

'Blackmail doesn't make me happy,' said Louis.

'Is that right?' Paul Kelly shrugged and headed towards the door. 'Well, we all have our little worries, don't we?'

Suddenly, rage filled Louis. 'Damn you to hell,' he yelled. 'When do I get my portrait back?'

Paul Kelly knocked his cigar ash onto the floor and stared at Louis with hard eyes. For the first time, Louis noticed that Kelly's irises were flecked with yellow. He shuddered despite himself. The man looked just like a tiger. A cunning, vicious tiger.

'*When* the job's done to my satisfaction, you'll

get your painting back,' snarled Paul Kelly. 'Not before.' He leaned so close the smell of scented hair oil filled Louis' nostrils. Then Kelly shoved him, sprawling, onto a chair in the corner. 'And don't you yell at me, kid, or I'll break your fingers one by one.'

That had been days ago. Now Louis stared down at the plate of cold, greasy chicken wings in front of him. The red juice from the buttered beets was almost the same colour as the stains on his fingers. The table that he had first seen covered with full bottles of ink, clean brushes and tools laid out in row, was scratched and stained. The bottles were empty, the tools were chipped and the brushes were worn out.

Louis' back ached from where he had sat for hours on end, putting finishing touches to the inked plates that had pressed out thousands of counterfeit bills. Now the printing press was silent and the stacks of bills had gone.

The door opened and a black man as square as a box stumped into the room. His name was Eugene Dipple and he was Kelly's master forger. There was no handwriting or signature that Eugene couldn't copy within seconds. During the time they had worked together, Eugene had taken a liking to Louis. He said they were the artists in the gang and they should stick together. Eugene said the rest of them were hooligans and scum.

Now Eugene grinned and held out a tiny piece of curled up paper. 'Your lucky day, kid. Word is to let you go.'

Louis stared down at the piece of paper. *Free Colbolt. Kelly's orders.* 'Who wrote this?'

'Who cares?' said Eugene. 'Not Kelly, that's for sure. I seen his writing a hundred times.' He fixed Louis with tired, red-rimmed eyes. 'But who am I to disobey orders?'

Louis' heart pounded in his chest.

Who was the message from? Could someone have found out where he had been taken?

Louis pushed the questions from his mind. There was no time to lose, he had to get out while he had the chance.

'Just a second, kid.' Eugene pulled a letter from his pocket and handed it to Louis. 'There's something I gotta tell you. I feel real bad about it but you gotta know.'

Louis looked at a letter written in his mother's handwriting, telling him of her illness and the financial problems she was suffering. He felt bile rising in his throat. It was exactly the same as the one he had received all those weeks ago. Now he realised that letter had been a fake. He thought he was going to be sick.

'I'm sorry, kid,' said Eugene. 'I just wrote what Kelly told me.'

Louis stared dumbly at him. 'But how did you know what my mother's handwriting *looked* like?'

Eugene shrugged. 'They gave me a letter from her. Must have stolen it from you.'

Louis stared into Eugene's square face. His nose had been broken so many times it sat on his face like a lump of putty. He wanted to feel rage but he couldn't. Eugene hadn't had to show him the letter and he knew Eugene wouldn't have had a choice when Kelly asked him to write it. No one refused Kelly's orders.

Through the open window, they heard the *clip clop*

of hooves and the jangle of a harness. Eugene looked into Louis' face. They both knew it could be Paul Kelly. 'You should run for it, kid. Seems to me you've got some clever friends.'

Louis shook Eugene's outstretched hands. 'Thanks. I owe you one.'

'You don't owe anyone anything except me.' A voice came from the doorway. Paul Kelly stood with two thickset men on either side of him. He nodded to one of them, who stepped forward with a wooden truncheon in his hand. A second later, Eugene slumped sideways onto the floor with what looked like a trickle of red ink spreading out from the back of his head.

'Take the kid to the cab,' snarled Paul Kelly.

Louis stepped backwards towards the table. 'I'm not going anywhere with you!' As he spoke, he grabbed two bottles of cleaning fluid and a handful of engraving pens with pointed nibs. He threw the fluid in the faces of the two men. They screamed and clutched their eyes as it burned them.

'Don't do anything stupid, Louis,' snarled Paul Kelly. 'You'll regret it.'

'What have I got to lose?' said Louis. An icy fury had taken hold of him. 'You've ruined my life!' Before Paul Kelly had a chance to move backwards, Louis dragged the sharp nibs down the side of his face.

The last thing Louis remembered was the look of surprise and fury in Paul Kelly's eyes. Then he felt a sharp blow on the back of his head and the world went black.

Down on the street, Mickey crouched in a doorway and waited. He felt cold and bad. Something had gone wrong. He was sure of it. The moment his gang had got word to him that the pigeon had been sent from Monk Hood's store with the message, he had run like a greyhound to the warehouse in Houston Street. The idea was to waylay Louis the moment he came through the door and take him to safety.

Then Paul Kelly had arrived in his cab and Mickey knew exactly what had happened. One of his gang had changed sides for an extra dollar. It was too late to try and figure out who it was.

The damage was done.

Now he watched Kelly walk out of the warehouse door, blood trickling down the side of his face. He looked as if he had been clawed by an animal. Mickey could see his eyes were sparking with rage. Then he watched as the unconscious Louis was carried out of the warehouse and dumped onto the floor of a cab.

Mickey trained every sense he had on Louis' body. He knew you could tell if a person was dead or alive by the way they were carried. A dead person was humped about like a carcass in a meat store. Mickey stared at Louis' white, white face and his shock of black hair. There was something about the body that was floppy not but lifeless.

Mickey was almost positive Louis was alive.

'Where to, boss?'

'The Silver Dollar,' called Kelly, stepping up into his own cab. 'Take him to the attic and tie him up tight.'

Mickey could have whooped for joy. Louis wasn't dead and now he knew where he was being taken. He waited until both cabs had turned the corner then he set off through the early dusk back to Washington Square.

Garth and Violet sat staring out of their window. Neither of them had spoken as the sky had changed from a bright afternoon blue to the dusky pinks and greys of early evening.

'Something's gone wrong,' muttered Violet. She pulled the Egyptian pendant out from around her neck and let it hang down the front of her blouse. 'Maybe we've run out of luck.'

'Cut the superstitious stuff,' said Garth sharply. He was worried sick about Mickey's safety as well as Louis' now. He looked up and saw the hurt on Violet's face. 'Sorry, Vi. I didn't mean it. You're right, something's gone wrong.'

'Mickey should have been back *hours* ago.' Violet held her head in her hands. 'Oh dear, Garth. I'm beginning to wonder if we've gone too far on our own.'

Before Garth could reply, the door opened and Mickey stepped into the room. He had a nasty bruise on one cheek as if someone had slapped him and he looked absolutely furious. 'Those cops!' he said in a choked voice. 'Arrested me, didn't they?' He held out the edges of the new corduroy jacket Mrs Murphy had given him. 'Accused me of stealing this, they did.' He threw himself down on the chair. 'Sorry. It took me ages to talk them round.'

Violet got up and poured out a big glass of grape juice from a jug on the table. Mrs Murphy had left a plateful of cookies that neither she nor Garth had touched. She picked up the plate and handed it to Mickey. 'Eat something. Then tell us what happened.'

All the cookies were finished by the time Mickey had told them everything he had seen.

'So he's being held at the Silver Dollar.' Garth shuddered. He would never forget the place. It had reeked of squalor and danger and evil. He knew for certain that he did not have the courage to go back.

'No point trying to pick him up tonight,' said Mickey. 'They must have hit him pretty hard and he'll be too groggy to follow me over the roofs.'

'It's too late for that,' said Violet quietly. 'It's

154

too dangerous for you and too dangerous for Louis. I think it's time we spoke to my father.'

'His Lordship!' gasped Mickey. He stared at Violet. 'Beggin' yer pardon, Miss Violet, but yer pa would never make it over dem roofs. It's bad enough for me.'

Violet laughed. 'I'm not suggesting that, Mickey. And you're right, Louis would never make it. I'm suggesting Father tells the police and they'll overrun the place.'

Mickey's eyes lit up. 'You mean a raid! Boy, would I like to be there!' His face darkened. 'Only one thing.'

'What?' asked Garth.

'Make sure his Lordship don't tell no bent cop. A lot of 'em are in Kelly's pay. Louis would be sunk if he told the wrong guy.'

Violet looked out through the window. It was dark now and the lights of the streetlamps sparkled on the leaves and turned them silver. Mickey was right. It was too late to do anything tonight. They would speak to her father in the morning.

'I'll write Father a note,' said Violet. 'And I'll

speak to Mrs Murphy this evening.' She smiled at Mickey. 'Just in case you need anything smoothed over.'

Mickey smiled back. 'Don't worry, Miss Vi. I've already done that. Everyting's smooth as honey.' He looked down at his jacket. 'Your fish face is even gonna make me a new jacket.'

Violet laughed again. 'You'll rule the world one day, Mickey. I'd put money on it.'

Mickey finished the last of the grape juice. 'So what's the plan?'

'We'll get word to you after we've spoken to Lord Percy,' said Garth. 'Around ten o'clock, maybe.'

'Suits me. I'll be in the pantry with the butler.' Mickey stood up to his full height and said proudly, 'I'm learning how to polish silver tomorrow.'

ELEVEN

The next morning Violet woke up feeling uneasy and out of sorts. She opened Homer's cage and held the little monkey to her face. He chirruped and buried his nose in her ear. Suddenly Violet felt afraid and for the first time, she wondered whether Louis was dead.

Homer felt her fear and plucked anxiously at her hair. 'Don't worry,' whispered Violet. 'I'm sure . . . yes, I'm sure, he's all right.' She lifted the lid off a pot full of nuts and pumpkin seeds and put a handful on the floor for Homer. 'Father will help us now.'

As Homer gobbled up the food, Violet put on her underclothes and petticoats and dressed in a soft wool skirt and red and white striped blouse. She pulled on a short, black, fitted jacket and tied up the laces on her walking boots. As she went into the hall, she realised she had dressed for a morning outside and yet she and Garth were supposed to be preparing a Latin translation exercise after breakfast. She shook her head, trying to get rid of the confusion that had taken hold of her.

Garth was standing at the bottom of the stairs. 'You look terrible,' he said.

'So do you.'

'I didn't sleep a wink.' Garth rubbed his hand over his face and hair. 'I feel sick. I'm so worried something terrible has happened to Louis.'

'Me too,' said Violet. 'I've gone over and over it. Why would Paul Kelly get rid of him? Anyway, you said you heard him promise Louis to give the portrait back in that street round the corner from Delmonico's.'

'Since when are Paul Kelly's promises worth believing?'

Violet went on speaking as if she hadn't heard him. 'And then there's Philip Van Horn. I think it's about time someone confronted him.' She put her hand on Garth's arm. 'Father will know what to do now.'

Garth shook his head miserably. 'I never thought I'd admit it, but I'll feel a lot better when we've talked to him.'

'Yup. And we'll both feel a lot better when we've had something to eat.' She smiled into Garth's unhappy face. 'I fancy waffles and syrup this morning. After porridge and kippers, of course.'

Garth managed to smile back. 'Food for the brain — and Mrs Murphy's waffles *are* the best in the world.'

Violet slipped her arm through Garth's. 'So what are we waiting for?'

Violet had it all worked out in her mind. She and Garth would walk into her father's study and tell them everything they knew. Lord Percy would listen carefully and jot notes on a piece of paper as they spoke. Afterwards, he would look proud but serious. He would make his usual subtle and brilliant suggestions and after that, everything would be sorted out and Louis would be rescued.

The moment Violet walked into her father's study, she knew she had got everything wrong.

Lord Percy was standing by the window, holding a letter in his hands. He didn't even look up when Violet and Garth came into the room. His face was white and frowning as if he couldn't believe what he was reading.

'Good God,' he muttered. 'Good God.' He shook his head, read the letter again and stared into middle distance. He didn't seem to have noticed that Violet and Garth were in the room.

Garth and Violet stared at each other. Neither of them had any idea what was going on but both of them could see that it looked like very bad news indeed. And the same name came into both their minds.

Louis Colbolt.

'Father,' said Violet, when she couldn't bear it a moment longer. 'I'm sorry to disturb you, but we have something very urgent and very serious to tell you.'

Lord Percy put down the letter and looked at her as if he hadn't heard a word she said.

'It's about Louis, Sir,' said Garth, trying to keep the desperation out of his voice. 'He's being held prisoner by a gangster called Paul Kelly.'

'Kelly kidnapped him after Daisy's reception,' continued Violet. 'He forced him to make counterfeit bills.' She swallowed and made herself meet her father's piercing grey eyes. 'We're sure Mr Van Horn is involved, but we don't know how.' Her last words tailed off as Lord Percy's eyes widened but still he said nothing.

'Father,' cried Violet, almost in tears. 'We need your help. Louis is in danger!'

There was a knock on the door and Dottie came in, carrying a tray with a cup and a pot of coffee. The silence in the room unnerved her and she set down the tray clumsily so that the cup clattered in its saucer.

For the first time Lord Percy spoke. It was as if the rattle of the china had brought him back to

161

his senses. He put the letter down on his desk. 'Bring two more cups, please, Dottie, and, ah, some chocolate biscuits.'

'Right away, Sir.' Dottie looked around at the three white faces, bobbed and hurried nervously from the room.

When the door closed, Lord Percy sat down and motioned for Garth and Violet to do the same. 'I'm sorry,' he said, in his usual even voice. 'I will explain what I can as soon as possible.' He looked at them both with a worried expression on his face. 'Now, it is terribly important that you tell me everything you know and how you found it out. Start from the very beginning.'

It didn't take Violet and Garth long to tell Lord Percy what had happened from the moment Garth had seen Louis climb into Paul Kelly's cab, to Mickey's report from outside the warehouse the night before.

'Louis must be rescued immediately, Father,' said Violet, trying hard to stop her voice from trembling. 'Mickey says Paul Kelly could do anything. Especially since it looked like Louis had struck him. His face was bleeding and Mickey said he had never seen him look so angry.'

Lord Percy picked up the letter he had been reading. 'It says here that Paul Kelly is dead,' he said slowly. 'His house was burned down last night. He was inside it.'

Violet stifled a shriek. But Garth held Lord Percy's eyes. Something in them made Garth feel chilled to the very core of his being.

'Who is that letter from, Sir?'

'Philip Van Horn, Garth. He says he shot Paul Kelly in his bed and burned down his house.'

'But why?' cried Violet. 'Father, what is going on?'

Lord Percy Winters took a deep breath and let it out slowly. 'I almost don't know where to begin,' he said. His eyes slid sideways to Garth. 'There are so many terrible things in this letter.'

Garth felt a chill run through him. What had been suspicions earlier, even though he hadn't been able to prove anything, were hardening into something else. Increasingly, Garth was sure that somehow his father had been involved with Paul Kelly. He clenched his fists and waited.

Violet leaned forward. 'So Daisy was right. There *was* something between Philip Van Horn and Paul Kelly?'

Lord Percy nodded. 'Apparently, many years ago they were partners in a despicable, dishonest and greedy business. At the time, no one had any idea what was going on. Paul Kelly employed thugs to frighten people into selling their houses on the Lower East Side, and Van Horn used his architect's training to turn them into tenements. The two of them split the profits. Philip Van Horn wanted the money to get accepted into New York Society. Paul Kelly wanted the money to build up an illegal empire. When they both got what they wanted, they dissolved the partnership. Van Horn made Kelly promise that he would never make contact again.' Lord Percy paused. 'Kelly kept that promise until two months ago, when he needed the skills of a forger and Louis fitted the bill.'

'So Mickey was right. It *was* Paul Kelly who told Mr Van Horn not to pay Louis,' said Violet.

Lord Percy nodded again. 'The purpose was to make poor Louis as desperate as possible so that he would have to accept Paul Kelly's offer.'

'And Paul Kelly stole the portrait to make sure of it.' Violet felt a surge of anger rush through her. 'What a truly evil man.'

'Yes.'

Garth looked into Lord Percy's face. He saw that there was something even more serious to come. 'Excuse me, Sir. I don't understand. Why did Van Horn write to *you*?'

A flicker of what looked like pain passed over Lord Percy's face. 'Because I am your guardian, Garth and, ah, Van Horn has given both you and Louis a substantial sum of money.'

'*Me*?' Garth was thunderstruck. 'What on earth for?' But even as he asked the question, Garth knew the answer. 'It's to do with my father, isn't it?'

Lord Percy nodded. 'I'm sorry, Garth. But yes, it is.'

Violet thought back to a rainy afternoon in November six months before, when her father and mother had announced that a young American called Garth Hudson would be coming to live with them. His father, Conrad, had been a good friend of

Lord Percy. When Conrad Hudson had disappeared earlier that year, Lord Percy honoured an agreement he had made with his friend to look after Garth in the unlikely event of his father's death. Since then Garth had become part of the family.

Violet stood up. 'I'll leave you both alone.'

Garth reached out and touched Violet's hand. 'No, stay. There's nothing your father can tell me that I wouldn't want you to hear.'

'Are you sure?'

'Yes.'

Violet sat down again and felt her heart hammering in her chest. The moment Garth had arrived, the two of them had got on very well. For Violet, the adventure they'd shared on the Nile had been the most exciting time in her life. And after it, she and Garth had become real friends.

Violet could hardly bear to look at Garth as his jaw clenched and unclenched even though he sat as still as a statue. She knew he had been disappointed not to find out the truth about his father while they were in New York. But he had tried as hard as he could and what with the disappearance of Louis, she had presumed he had decided to let the question rest.

Now that Garth was about to find out the truth about his father, Violet felt sick to her stomach. How could a man like Philip Van Horn have anything to do with Garth's father, who had been a respected lawyer and, according to her mother, a retiring man, not much interested in New York Society?

Lord Percy walked over to where Garth was sitting and pulled up a chair beside him. 'What I'm about to tell you is very difficult. I can only say that we are your family now and we will do everything we can to help you.'

Garth stared down at his hands. 'What does Van Horn have to do with my father?'

'It's not just Van Horn. Paul Kelly was involved, too.'

Violet bit her hand not to cry out. Now she understood what her father was going to say. She looked to where Garth sat frozen and waiting. If he had guessed, too, she would never have known it. His face stayed exactly the same.

Lord Percy caught the look in his daughter's eyes and turned away. It seemed as if he didn't know where to begin. 'You remember what I've just told you about Van Horn and Kelly's business buying up houses and turning them into tenements?'

Garth nodded.

'It was a common practice then and everyone involved was corrupt. The police took bribes. So did the city officials. Your father knew what Van Horn and Kelly were doing. He was trying to make a case against them. The problem was that no one dared give evidence. Every time Conrad managed to track someone down who would talk, that person mysteriously disappeared.'

Lord Percy got up again and picked up the letter on his desk. 'Van Horn says here that long after their, in his words, *shameful association* was over, Paul Kelly's gang had got control not only of the housing in the Lower East Side but were also running the water front and the sweat shops that paid immigrant labour slave wages. As Kelly grew more powerful, your father grew more determined to bring him to justice.'

Lord Percy looked up. 'Then Conrad received a letter from a retired policeman whose conscience had finally caught up with him – even if it was twenty years later. At any rate, the man wrote down his part in the corruption and with his evidence your father began to assemble a case. All this happened about two years ago.'

Lord Percy put down the letter and went back over to Garth and Violet. 'Unfortunately, before Paul Kelly could be brought to trial both the policeman and your father disappeared. And the statement the policeman had written was never found.' Lord Percy swallowed. 'Van Horn believes your father was murdered and his body put in the river.'

Dumped! You mean dumped! thought Violet angrily. *With a concrete block tied to his foot!*

Outside the window, a milk wagon rattled to a stop. There was a clash of metal churns as the delivery man dragged them off the back of the cart and let them slip onto the ground. A horse's harness jingled and faded away.

Garth didn't look up from his lap. In some ways

he was relieved to have his suspicions confirmed at last. 'At least Kelly's dead,' he said. His voice was barely more than a whisper. 'And at least I know what probably happened to my father.'

Lord Percy put his arm around Garth's shoulder and held him hard. 'I promise you, Garth, we will do everything we can to find Van Horn. Pinkertons Detective Agency are on the case already.'

Lord Percy handed Garth the letter. 'Read the last paragraph.'

Garth stared hard at the words, which were blurring in front of his eyes. *I hope that by telling you what I have, I will have gone some way to make amends. However, it is not my intention to give myself up. And you can be sure I will never be found. Philip Van Horn.*

Garth handed back the letter. 'Would Pinkertons' men be able to find Louis, too?'

Lord Percy shook his head. 'That could risk Louis' safety. Kelly's men would panic if Pinkertons raided the Silver Dollar. And as you said to me earlier, Louis may well be disposable now.' Lord Percy pulled the servants' bell rope. There was a muffled clang from the basement floor of the house. 'I believe our only hope lies with your Mickey Gallagher.'

Two minutes later, Mrs Murphy stood in front of them. Her eyes were red and her hands twisted and turned as she spoke. Dottie had told her something dreadfully serious was happening in his Lordship's study and when Mickey had been sent for, she immediately presumed that he was in trouble. Now Mrs Murphy was beside herself. She had to tell his Lordship that Mickey was nowhere to be found and it looked as if his bed hadn't been slept in. She had no idea where he could be.

For a moment, no one spoke. They had all been depending on the wits of the young street urchin and now, when they needed him most, he had disappeared. In the silence, a shadow seemed to creep across the room. Violet looked out of the window. The pale morning light was turning darker by the minute. Lord Percy went over and closed the windows, which had been opened to let in the warm spring air.

Violet shivered. Suddenly the room felt cold and damp.

Garth stared out across the square. The clouds had thickened and it was as if a wad of grey cotton wool was blocking out the sky.

'There's a blizzard coming,' said Garth. His voice sounded as if he was speaking from the bottom of a well. He turned to Violet. 'Remember what I said in the Soda Fountain? There's always one more.'

Violet nodded but couldn't speak. In the dull light from the window, only she could see the tears that glistened on Garth's cheeks.

TWELVE

Mickey sat in the coal shed in Paul Kelly's backyard and chewed his fingernails to the quick. For the first time in his life he didn't know what to do. Everything was going wrong and happening faster than he could have ever imagined. He forced his mind backwards to try and make sense of things.

As soon as had he left Garth and Violet the previous evening, every instinct in Mickey's body had told him to look for Louis in Paul Kelly's house. The more they had talked, the more Mickey was bothered by something that didn't add up. Why would Paul Kelly take Louis back to the Silver Dollar? It didn't make sense. Someone would be bound to notice and word would get around. Everyone knew Louis had been brought in to put the final touches to the fake notes and the rumour Mickey had heard was that Louis had done a brilliant job. Even so, Mickey also knew that Kelly would make good and sure that Louis understood his usefulness was over. That would make him easier to frighten. Then the rescue attempt had gone wrong at the warehouse. Now Mickey realised that Kelly knew he was being overheard when he gave orders to take Louis to the Silver Dollar. He knew someone like Mickey would be waiting around the corner to help Louis escape as soon as Eugene received the carrier pigeon's message. And Mickey had fallen for it − hook, line and sinker. When the cabs were out of sight, Kelly had changed his orders.

Mickey groaned out loud. It wasn't until he was back in Washington Square, creeping across the gleaming, empty kitchen and down the corridor to his cupboard of a bedroom, that he had pieced it all together. It was thinking of his silver-polishing lesson the next morning that had helped him realise the truth. Mr Edgar, the butler, had made it very plain that Mickey was going to start learning on silver plate. The really valuable pieces would come later when he proved he could do a good job.

Kelly must have realised that he had found a brilliant forger in Louis. There was no way he was going to risk losing him. There would be more valuable work to do later.

It had taken Mickey two hours to cross the city to Lower Broadway, where Kelly lived. Then, sure enough, when he'd inched up the guttering pipe of the mansion and climbed in an open window, he had found Louis chained to the wall in a studio in the attic.

Poor Louis! He had no idea whether the kid was there to kill him or rescue him. And it had used up all of Mickey's persuasive powers to stop him from yelling as he unpicked the chain's padlock. Then, just as Mickey led Louis back down the stairs, clouds of choking smoke had risen up through the house from the bottom floor.

There had been no time to lose. Mickey had run

into the first bedroom he could find, ripped two pillowcases from the bed and soaked them in a pitcher of water. Then he had shown Louis how to cover his mouth and nose and crawl along the floor behind him, motioning him to keep as close as he could.

A minute later, Louis was halfway out of the window and getting a foothold on the guttering when Mickey suddenly remembered the second part of his mission.

'Be in de coal shed at the end of the yard,' Mickey had hissed. 'Or you'll be a dead man for sure.' And Louis had nodded. He seemed to have realised that if Mickey had come to kill him, he would have done it already. As Louis slid down the wall, Mickey went back into the house.

Which is when he heard a gun go off and saw Philip Van Horn run from a bedroom and down the stairs. By now the smoke was thick and choking. Mickey ran, bent double, along the corridor to the room Van Horn had just left.

Under a gold satin bedspread embroidered with the letters PK lay a hunched shape. A red stain was spreading from under the bedspread and blood was dripping onto the floor. Mickey quickly crossed the carpeted floor and pulled back a corner of the bedspread. The man in the bed was not Paul Kelly. Van Horn had shot someone called Curly Joe. Everyone in the Bowery knew Curly Joe and Mickey had overheard a conversation in the Silver Dollar about how he had tried to double-cross Kelly. Now Curly Joe's hands were tied behind his back and despite the stinking smoke and smell of cordite from the gun, the faintest whiff of chloroform wafted from a rag by his head.

There was a shattering of glass as windows exploded on the floor below. Any minute now, flames would spread up the staircase and Mickey's escape route would be blocked. He flipped the bedspread back over Curly Joe's grey face and looked around the room.

So far Mickey's instincts about Kelly had been right. Now he was putting them to the test for the last time. He was sure Kelly was keeping Louis' portrait in his bedroom. It was where he kept all of his trophies. He'd boasted as much time and time again. Also, a bedroom would be the perfect place to hide a large portrait, as no one but Kelly and a house maid would ever use the room. Mickey looked around him. Sure enough, the room was decorated in a show-offish, almost childish way. Everywhere there were self-portraits and montages of newspaper cuttings, with Kelly's photograph in the middle. Most were stories of crimes that had never been solved. It was as if Kelly was laughing at the men who couldn't enforce the law in New York.

Mickey pulled open chests of drawers and mahogany cupboards but couldn't find anything that looked like a portrait-shaped parcel. He looked behind the curtain and even pulled up a corner of the carpet where it seemed lumpy and raised.

Nothing.

More windows shattered and there was a crash from below as if a wall had fallen down. The bedroom shook and a full-length portrait of Paul Kelly, dressed in a top hat and tails, tipped to one side. Mickey turned around. The edge of a flat brown parcel suddenly appeared from behind the frame!

There was a great whooshing sound. The fire had spread up the stairs. As fast as he could, Mickey yanked the heavy picture from the wall. As it fell, the flat brown parcel dropped onto the floor. Mickey tore away a piece of the packing. It was the portrait! He grabbed a towel, dunked it in the pitcher of water that stood by Kelly's bed and wrapped it round the parcel.

Then he ran for the door.

By now, the smoke in the corridor was almost unbearable. Mickey dropped to his knees and crawled as fast as he could, dragging the portrait behind him. He headed back along the corridor to the room with the open window.

As Mickey reached the coal shed, the police and firemen arrived. He should have felt relief but as soon as he saw them, he felt his stomach go cold. They were all from the Silver Dollar. They were Paul Kelly's men.

Now Mickey rubbed his hands over his face and stared at the house that was engulfed in sparks and flames. It had all happened so fast.

'Blessed Mary,' muttered Mickey to himself. 'Dat

was too close for comfort.' He crossed himself and wiped a filthy sleeve across his face. 'Dat's it. I'm goin' straight now.'

Beside him, Louis Colbolt rubbed at the red welts on his wrists where the chain had cut into his skin. He looked into Mickey's blackened face. Only the whites of his eyes could be seen in the dark night. Louis shivered and fought an overwhelming urge to scream. 'Who are you?' he croaked. 'How did you know I was here?'

'Name's Mickey Gallagher.' Mickey held out his rough, grimy hand. 'Kitchen boy to the Winters' household. As for findin' yus, I knows Kelly. He's a thief, a liar and a murderer.'

Louis stared at the white eyes in the skinny, sooty face. If this urchin really did work for Lord Percy's family, could it be that he knew Garth or even Violet? For the first time in what seemed like months, Louis let something like hope flutter into his mind. 'Do you know Violet and Garth?' he whispered.

'That's why I'm here,' said Mickey. 'Risked my bleeding neck for you, I 'ave.' He shrugged. 'Mind you, I'd do anything for Miss Violet, and for Mrs Murphy too, 'a course.'

'Who's Mrs Murphy?'

'The cook.'

Louis shook his head. His world had turned upside down and inside out so many times recently, he didn't know what to believe. He looked at the burning house and again fought the urge to scream. 'I'd have been burned alive if it hadn't been for you.'

Mickey patted Louis' shaking body with his thin sooty hand. 'Lucky for you, den, wasn't it?'

There was a tremendous crash as part of the roof fell in and sent up another brilliant spray of sparks into the night.

Firemen were running around, aiming great canvas hoses on the flames – but it was too late. The house was lost. As Louis and Mickey watched, two men rushed across the yard carrying a stretcher. There was a body underneath the blanket.

'I hope that devil rots in hell,' snarled Louis in a voice he barely recognised as his own.

Mickey followed his eyes. 'And which devil would dat be?'

'Paul Kelly,' cried Louis. He stared at Mickey. 'You know him. You said you did.'

'Oh, I know 'im, all right,' said Mickey. 'That's why I know that stiff ain't Paul Kelly.'

'What?' Louis' voice rose above the roar of the flames.

'For gawd's sake, keep yer mouth shut,' said Mickey in a fierce whisper. 'Those ain't no ordinary firemen out there. And those ain't no ordinary cops, neither. They's all working for Kelly and if they find us, we've 'ad it.'

'How do you know?'

'Will ya stop askin' me questions, ya daft lump,' snapped Mickey. 'I knows 'em all. Now, listen. We gotta wait here till morning. Ain't nothing else for it.'

He pulled a couple of hessian coal sacks from a pile in the corner and threw them at Louis. 'We might as well get some kip.' Then, without waiting for a reply, he curled up against a filthy coal sack and fell asleep.

Mickey had no idea what time it was when he woke

but the moment he looked out the door, he could see a blizzard was coming. The sky was the colour of lead and the air was heavy with a feeling of snow. He looked quickly behind him. Louis was still asleep.

'Jaysus,' muttered Mickey, looking back through the door. 'A bleedin' blizzard.' He shook his head. 'All they'll have to do is follow our footsteps.' He peered around the entrance to the coal shed. Luckily it was hidden by a pair of overgrown spruce trees. Paul Kelly was obviously no gardener.

The house was a smoking ruin with three walls standing and half a dozen blackened timbers sticking into the sky. Everything was quiet but, as Mickey let his eyes move slowly around, he saw the tops of two plaid caps sticking up over a brick wall by a side entrance.

Kelly's men. Mickey was sure of it. Somehow he and Louis were going to have to get past them.

Louis grunted and shifted in the corner. Mickey shook him awake and whispered in his ear. 'Listen to me and don' say nuffin'. There's two of Kelly's bully-boys by the side door and if they 'ear us, we're dead meat. There be more of 'em soon so we gotta get outta here.' He reached behind him and put the flat parcel into Louis' hands. 'An' there's this to look after, too, so we don' wanna get caught.'

Louis stared at the shape. For a moment, he didn't speak. Then his voice came out in a low squawk. 'Is this my portrait?'

Mickey nodded and to his astonishment, Louis' shoulders heaved. It looked as if he was going to burst into sobs.

'Shush, ya great booby,' hissed Mickey. 'Or we'll *both* be 'owling proper in a minute!'

THIRTEEN

Violet couldn't believe her eyes. What had begun as a fluttering of flakes past the window had turned into a white curtain of snow. The view of the hedge and the square had disappeared completely. Violet turned to Garth, fighting to keep her voice under control. 'We've got to get Louis,' she muttered. 'Anything could have happened to him.'

'All we can do is wait,' said Lord Percy firmly. 'It would be foolhardy to go out in this blizzard.' He pointed beyond the window to where the world had turned white. 'Surely you can see that for yourself.'

Garth looked at Violet's miserable face. 'There's always Mickey,' he said in a low voice.

'What do you mean?'

'I think he's gone after Louis on his own. I mean, he knows better than any of us how dangerous Paul Kelly is, or was.' Garth shrugged. 'At any rate, I think one of Mickey's gang must have got some information to him last night.'

'One of Mickey's gang betrayed Louis,' said Violet flatly.

At that moment, the door opened and Lady Eleanor walked into the room. Daisy Van Horn was slumped on her arm. Lady Eleanor was still dressed in a morning gown of pearl-grey satin edged with white down. And her glossy golden hair was piled loosely on top of her head. Beside her, Daisy Van Horn shivered inside a thin blue cloak with a fringed shawl pulled over her wet, bedraggled hair. Her head and shoulders were covered in snow and her white kid boots were soaked and muddy. She looked as if she had thrown on the first clothes she could find and run all the way from her parents' house to Washington Square.

'Percy,' said Lady Eleanor smoothly. 'I have sent the footman to fetch Miss Van Horn's belongings from her parents' house immediately.' Lady Eleanor paused and fixed her husband with a look that Violet knew only too well. Her mother would not be countermanded. 'Miss Horn will be staying with us for the foreseeable future.'

Lord Percy raised his eyebrows. He knew his wife had no knowledge of Philip Van Horn's letter, yet clearly something had happened that was connected to it. 'What on earth is the matter, my dear?'

'It's outrageous,' murmured Lady Eleanor, her cream-coloured skin blushing the faintest pink. 'Enid Van Horn has simply abandoned dear Daisy. She left this morning for her family house in Connecticut.' Lady Eleanor turned to the window. 'Although in this weather, I'd say she'll be regretting her decision.' She dropped her voice to a whisper and leaned across to her husband. 'The woman's out of her mind, Percy. And as for Van Horn. Well, a cad is all I can say.'

'He's worse than a cad,' cried Daisy suddenly. Violet watched her mother's complexion turn from pink to rose. 'Mother says he's dishonest and deceitful and no better than a common criminal.

Mother says he has disgraced us all and she can never set foot in New York again.'

Daisy buried her head in her hands but it was as if her words had settled her mind. Her shoulders stopped shaking.

'But what of you, Daisy?' asked Lord Percy kindly. 'Surely your mother hasn't left you alone?'

A fierceness that Violet had seen before came into Daisy's face. 'My mother is a snob, Lord Percy. She cares about nothing except herself and her place in Society. All I found this morning was a note to say that she would be in the country until further notice. The servants had orders to cover the furniture with dust sheets. There will be only a skeleton staff left in the house. She has made no arrangements for me at all.'

Daisy fixed her china-doll eyes on Lord Percy's face. 'My life is with Louis, now.'

For the second time in one morning, Violet saw her father discomfited. He cleared his throat and appeared to be choosing his words carefully. 'Daisy, you should understand that as yet we have no word of Louis. Of course, we are hopeful he is safe and that he will be found very soon.'

Daisy stared at him as if he was mad. She had been sure as she ran all the way to Washington Square that the police would have arrested that foul man, Paul Kelly, and charged him with kidnapping. What's more, she had been positive that Louis would be here, waiting for her. Daisy let out a single, high-pitched scream and slumped to the ground in a dead faint.

'Mr Wannamaker, my Lord.' Dottie stood outside the open door to announce the visitor. Then she stared in horror at the scene in front of her. Violet had Daisy's head in her lap. Lady Eleanor was passing her the bottle of smelling salts she always carried in an embroidered purse around her waist. Garth, purple with embarrassment, was desperately tugging Daisy's skirt downwards to cover the petticoats and bloomers that her unexpected fall had revealed and Lord Percy was standing with his eyes wide and staring and his hands to his face.

'Damnable weather you've arranged for me, Percy, eh what?' Herbert Wannamaker crashed into the room like a walrus on wagon wheels. He seemed totally oblivious to the sight of Daisy on the floor and grabbed Lord Percy by the hand. 'Never seen the like of it! A blizzard in April, for heaven's sake!'

Lady Eleanor, who had composed herself with the speed of a striking cobra, glided towards him and extended a slender hand.

'Dear Eleanor!' spluttered Herbert Wannamaker. He took her hand and held it to his lips. 'As beautiful as ever.'

'Herbert! What a surprise! We were expecting you at the end of the week.' Lady Eleanor smiled graciously and backed towards the door. 'Please excuse my *déshabillé*.'

Herbert Wannmaker laughed. 'It is I who should apologise. I was indeed supposed to arrive on Friday but a first-class cabin became available on an earlier ship, so I took it.' He turned to Lord Percy. 'Besides, I have to admit, Percy, since receiving your cable my curiosity to meet young Colbolt and see his work was quite getting the better of me.'

He looked over to where Violet was still bent over Daisy. 'And you must be Violet. Your father has told me so much about you.'

Violet couldn't stop a smile. The whole scene was like something out of a French farce. 'Indeed I am.' She touched Daisy's arm. 'And this is Daisy Van Horn. The uh, subject of Louis Colbolt's most recent portrait.'

Herbert Wannamaker twirled the ends of his enormous handlebar moustache and stared at Daisy's waxen doll face. 'Mmm. A pretty thing. A trifle indisposed, I see.'

Violet decided to follow Herbert Wannamaker's example, acting as if Daisy's prone figure was nothing unusual. 'I hope your crossing was calm.'

'Like a mill pond, dear girl.'

'How fortunate.' Violet turned towards Garth. 'May I introduce my father's ward, Garth Hudson?'

Garth took his cue from Violet and acted as if nothing strange was happening. Everything else was crazy, so why not? It was almost a relief. He stepped forward and shook hands. He knew he was looking at the person who would decide Louis' future, should there be a future to decide, and he felt an immediate affection for the huge, thunderous man.

Lord Percy had the feeling that he was the only sane person in the room. No one, not even Violet now, seemed to be taking any notice of the fact that Daisy Van Horn was still lying insensible on the floor.

'Violet, my dear,' he said in a choked voice. 'Do think you might ring for a lady's maid? I believe Daisy might be more comfortable lying, ah, on a bed.'

At this moment, Daisy's eyes fluttered open. She groaned and Violet helped her to a sofa.

Herbert Wannamaker crossed over to her and held out a hand the size of a huge flipper. 'Herbert Wannamaker, my dear.'

Daisy knew exactly who he was. She and Louis had talked of no one else for weeks. But now Louis was nowhere to be found. Maybe he was dead. It was all too much for Daisy. She tried to open her mouth to explain but no words came out. Instead she groaned and slumped sideways onto the sofa.

A gust of cold air suddenly blew into the room, bringing with it a sprinkling of snow. Everyone watched in complete silence as a heavy sash window was heaved up and Louis Colbolt climbed awkwardly into the room. Mickey clambered in behind him, manhandling a flat brown parcel.

No one spoke. No one even shut the window against the snow which was piling up on the Turkish carpet on the study floor.

Mickey looked around in utter astonishment. It was as if everyone in the room was made of stone. Finally his eyes fixed on Violet. 'Stone de crows, Miss Violet! Ain't nobody pleased to see us?'

Paul Kelly sat back on the plush yellow seats of his hansom cab and took a swig from a flask of bourbon he kept in his inside jacket pocket. He pulled back the ruffled satin curtain and looked out of the window. Snow was still falling thick and fast. Not the best day to be travelling but not the worst either. The blizzard meant the roads were empty and that suited him perfectly. It would be a long, slow ride to New Orleans, but what matter? He had all the time in the world. Paul Kelly smiled to himself and took another swig from his flask. No one would be following him because by now most of his enemies would assume he was dead. Philip Van Horn had made sure of that.

Or at least, he *thought* he had. Until he had run from Kelly's burning house straight into the arms of Kelly's henchman. Kelly smiled again. He couldn't resist it. He had always been able to outwit Van Horn. His driver, Sidney, had been in Kelly's pay for months. Information was always useful to Kelly, so as soon as he heard stories of the arguments and accusations after the reception at Delmonico's, he knew it was only a matter of time before Van Horn would try to get his revenge. Then Sidney had reported that his employer had ordered a large quantity of paraffin from his hardware supplier. And that he had been seen destroying personal papers and had ordered his valet to pack him a bag. That had been last night and Kelly had guessed with the wily sense of a successful criminal that Van Horn was coming to kill him and burn down his house. Putting an end to his enemy and then setting fire to everything his enemy owned was just the sort of melodramatic gesture that Van Horn would want to make. Particularly when he knew that the portrait that had caused so much trouble would be destroyed too.

So Kelly had set his trap. If he caught his quarry, so much the better. If he didn't, he would bide his time. Kelly left orders to leave his house unguarded and the ground floor windows unlocked. His three servants were given the night off. He knew that it would never occur to Van Horn to question the fact that he could break in so easily and find the house empty. He was too used to the soft life for that. As for Curly Joe, well, anyone who tried to double-cross Paul Kelly had it coming to him. And Kelly had guessed rightly that the cowardly Van Horn wouldn't check before he fired the gun that the man asleep in his bed was the man he wanted to kill. The only detail that had gone wrong was losing Louis Colbolt. Kelly had given express orders for him to be removed and taken to a safe house but the man entrusted with the job had been knifed in an alleyway.

Kelly frowned for the first time that morning. It was a pity about Louis. He was a fine counterfeiter and, with experience and Kelly's guidance, he could have become a master forger. His death was all Philip Van Horn's fault and Kelly felt no guilt about the orders he had given his gang when they grabbed Van Horn leaving the burning house.

Kelly tried to imagine what must have gone through Van Horn's mind as he lay trussed up in the back of the cab with a concrete block tied to his feet. He wondered whether Van Horn's life had passed through his mind in the seconds it took Kelly's men to throw him from the quayside into the river. What could it be like to feel the weight of the concrete block dragging you down through the black, icy water?

Kelly shuddered and drank some more bourbon. It was past imagining. Better for him to think of his new life in the South. He would have to change his name, of course, and dye his hair. Silver seemed appropriate. Perhaps he would grow a moustache and sideburns. At any rate, with the hundreds and thousands of counterfeit dollars stacked in boxes in the floor of his cab, he could become a proper Southern gentleman virtually overnight. Nobody asked questions if you had enough money.

At that moment Kelly's dreams of sipping rum punches on the pillared verandah of his white Southern mansion were interrupted. His driver, Tortoise Molloy, so-called because of his long, loose-skinned neck, knocked sharply three times on the roof of the cab. It was a signal that something was wrong. Kelly tapped back twice, telling Molloy to stop.

The cab pulled up sharply. Molloy swung down and pulled open the door. 'Roadblock, Boss. Whaddyawanna do?' He pointed ahead to where a cluster of police wagons were straddled over the main street under the steel girders of a bridge.

Paul Kelly frowned. Why on earth would there be a roadblock on a day like this? They couldn't possibly be looking for him. But his skin crawled with a cold, clammy, sixth sense. They *were* looking for him. Paul Kelly shook his head to clear his thoughts. But how could they know he was alive? The only person left in the house had been Louis, and he had gone up in flames with Curly Joe.

'We ain't got much time, Boss,' said Molloy in a

husky voice. 'No one on the road but us and here we are stopped. Doesn't look good.'

'Where are we?'

'Beside the East River, towards the bridge into Brooklyn.' Molloy paused. 'We could pull off ahead and take the track by the water. It's bad in snow so they wouldn't be expectin' that. Then we could cut back into town and lose 'em.'

'What's the risk?'

Molloy shrugged and looked back at the horse. 'We got a good nag. Sure-footed. Yeah. We'll be OK.'

Kelly thought of the money hidden in the cab. If they were stopped by cops that weren't in his pay, they'd put him in jail for the rest of his life. Every judge in New York wanted his skin. 'Do what it takes,' he muttered. Then he pulled up the window and sat back in the cab.

Tortoise Molloy whipped the horse forwards and pulled the reins sharply to the right. The cab lurched onto the bumpy narrow track and kept going. As soon as the police saw where the mysterious black cab was going, the air filled with clanging bells.

For the first time in his life, an edgy panic gripped Kelly's stomach and he felt bile rise in his throat. He swallowed the rest of the flask to take away the taste, then he pulled down the window and stuck his head out into the thick, falling snow. 'Lose 'em!' he yelled at the top of his voice.

A gun went off behind them and the noise of the shot ricocheted under the bridge. After that, it seemed to Paul Kelly that everything happened very slowly. The blast of the gun made the horse shy and swerve sideways. It twisted its harness and the wooden shafts connected to the cab snapped. It was the narrowest point of the track, only feet away from a rocky embankment that led down to the water. The cab crashed on its side, bounced once and tumbled over the rocks into the freezing East River.

If it hadn't been for the weight of the counterfeit notes hidden in heavy wooden boxes in the floor of the cab, Paul Kelly might have had a chance to swim free. He had learned to swim as a boy in Ireland a nd he was proud of it. But as the cab fell over the rocks, the door caved in and he was trapped.

Within seconds the weight of the boxes dragged the cab and Paul Kelly down through the icy water, just as the concrete block had pulled Philip Van Horn through the same freezing river a few hours before.

FOURTEEN

Herbert Wannamaker stood with a glass of champagne in his hand and stared at the portrait in front of him.

Violet could tell that he was as taken aback by it as everyone else had been at the reception in Delmonico's.

'Extraordinary,' muttered Herbert Wannamaker, half aloud. 'An all-seeing spectre. Yet flesh and blood.

'Extraordinary,' he said again.

On the other side of the room, Lord Percy and Garth stood together, talking in low voices. They were the only other people left in the room. It was as if the chaotic French farce that had been played out earlier was finished. Now the serious side of things had taken over again.

Louis and Daisy had been escorted upstairs for baths and a change of clothes. Mickey had been dragged downstairs for the same reason.

Violet smiled to herself as she remembered her dear codfish's face when she had set eyes on Mickey after being summoned to her father's study. She could see it had taken all the little French-woman's control not to throw her arms around him and clasp him to her bosom. As it was, when they were excused, she grabbed Mickey's hand and dragged him from the room, admonishing him all the way in fluent French. What a worry he was to them! Breakfast was waiting! The hot tub was almost full in the wash house! Mickey's protesta-tions that he was allergic to anything to do with hot tubs were studiously ignored and Violet could see from his grimy, grinning face that he was delighted with all the attention he was getting.

Now her father's serious-sounding voice broke into her thoughts. Violet left Herbert Wannamaker staring in amazement at the portrait and crossed to where her father and Garth had sat down at the desk.

'Let me make quite sure of this,' said Lord Percy as Violet joined them. 'Mickey has told you that the man killed in the fire was not Paul Kelly.'

Garth nodded. 'Mickey saw Mr Van Horn leave the room with a gun. He must have already set fire to the ground floor. When Mickey went into the bedroom, he pulled back the bedclothes to check. The dead man was someone he'd heard of, called Curly Joe. Apparently this man double-crossed Kelly.' Garth paused. 'Mickey said it smelled as if the man had been drugged with chloroform.'

Lord Percy shook his head. 'So,' he continued, trying to keep the disgust out of his voice. 'We must now believe that both Kelly and Van Horn are at large.' Garth and Violet nodded and watched as Lord Percy took a piece of headed paper from his escritoire and began to write rapidly across the thick white vellum. 'I'll send this information to Pinkertons Detective Agency immediately.'

'Do you think they'll catch them?' asked Violet.

It was impossible to imagine Philip Van Horn being handcuffed and led to a police wagon.

'If they can't, nobody can.' Lord Percy sealed the note and rang for Ed Tattle, the footman. Ed's uniform was already wet and his boots muddy. He had just returned from fetching Daisy Van Horn's belongings.

'I am sorry to send you out again.' Lord Percy saw Ed's face fall at the sight of the sealed envelope held out towards him. 'But please, do hurry, this is very, very urgent.'

Ed bowed. 'I'll go as fast as I can, my Lord.'

'Good man,' said Lord Percy. He reached into his pocket and handed over a dollar bill. 'Buy yourself a hot breakfast on the way back.'

Twenty minutes later, Lord Percy's note was in the hands of Dick Tracker, the head of Pinkertons' downtown office on Broadway.

Dick Tracker took one look at its contents, gave a low whistle of astonishment, then grabbed his hat and coat and set off to the Central New York Police Station. If Paul Kelly was indeed alive and the whole house fire had been an elaborate cover-up, then Dick Tracker knew that Kelly would be trying to get out of the city as soon as possible. He broke into a run along the slushy, slippery sidewalks. In this kind of weather, only the main roads would be passable and Kelly would not be expecting any trouble. If everyone moved fast, they could set up roadblocks on all the roads and the bridges out of the city. Tracker knew that there wasn't a decent cop in New York who didn't want to see Kelly behind bars. It was their only chance.

Louis Colbolt's mind was spinning. He didn't know whether it was the champagne or Herbert Wannamaker's offer of his patronage and a studio in Paris. Perhaps it was the look on Daisy's face when he had asked her to marry him and she had said yes. Perhaps it was the gut-churning debt of gratitude he felt towards Mickey Gallagher.

Louis looked over to where Mickey stood, flanked on one side by Mrs Murphy and on the other by Madame Poisson. The filthy face and tousled hair had disappeared. Mickey was no longer the skinny street boy who had picked the padlock on his chains and led him out of the burning house to the safety of the coal shed. And later over the roofs to safety.

Now Mickey stood proudly in brand-new corduroy trousers, new leather boots, a dark blue shirt and a red woollen waistcoat with real horn buttons. His face was scrubbed clean and his hair had been cut and brushed smooth. For the first time, Mickey looked like the young boy he really was. Louis slipped over to Lord Percy's desk and took out a piece of plain paper. Then, reaching for a pencil, he began to sketch Mickey's face as quickly as he could.

Daisy Van Horn stood with Lady Eleanor and felt at any moment that her heart might burst with happiness. Opposite them, Herbert Wannamaker was beaming. 'Of course, I would be delighted to escort you both back to Paris. I shall order my man to reserve a first-class state room for the new Mr and Mrs Colbolt.' He held the ends of Daisy's slender fingers and squeezed them in his great, wide hand. 'It will be a honour, I assure you.'

Daisy was so overwhelmed she didn't know what to say.

'Dear Herbert,' said Lady Eleanor smoothly. 'You are so kind. But you must understand that preparations for Daisy's wedding will take a little while.' She turned to Daisy and smiled gently. 'Even though I understand your reasons for wanting a simple ceremony.'

It seemed to Daisy that on this, the happiest day of her life so far, all she could do was cry. Earlier, Lady Eleanor had come into her bedroom and sat down beside her. She was delighted to learn from Louis that they were to be married, but Lady Eleanor was concerned that Daisy consulted her mother about the wedding, even though Enid Van Horn had been happy to abandon her. Lady Eleanor had taken Daisy's hand and held it firmly. 'Some things have to be done properly, Daisy. It's as important for Louis as for you. Of course, in the circumstances, you can choose a simple ceremony, but these things are not arranged overnight.' Lady Eleanor had paused and stared at the row of tiny, mother-of-pearl buttons that fastened the sleeve of her sea-green taffeta dress. 'Also, I think you must come to terms with the fact that your father may never be found.'

Daisy had looked up and Lady Eleanor was almost startled. There was a fierceness in Daisy's eyes that she had never noticed before. 'Lady Eleanor,' Daisy replied in a low voice. 'It would be better if my father were to be found dead.'

Lady Eleanor had turned scarlet and twisted her emerald engagement ring round and round on her finger. She knew she ought to remonstrate with Daisy but how could she? The very same thought had occurred to her.

She stood up. 'I will ring for my maid to dress your hair,' she said simply. Then she quickly left the room.

Dick Tracker had never visited a house as grand as the one he now stood in front of in Washington Square. Despite himself, he felt nervous, not least because of what he had to tell Lord Percy Winters. Through the large glass windows on the ground floor, he saw a group of people in a room to the right of the front door. Dick stared in astonishment. The snow had stopped falling now and he could see in quite clearly. It looked as if there was some kind of celebration going on. Everyone's face was bright and excited. A servant was pouring out champagne.

Suddenly a girl appeared at the window and Dick Tracker found himself staring into a pair of dark blue eyes in a long serious face. He felt at once that the girl knew who he was and what he had come for. She stared a second longer as if she was trying to make up her mind what to do, then she turned and spoke to an older man who Dick Tracker recognised as Lord Percy.

His detective's experience told him to wait and not to ring the bell. He made the right decision. The door was opened by Lord Percy himself and he was ushered quietly into the house and taken down the corridor to the drawing room. A moment later, they were joined by Lady Eleanor, Garth, Mickey, Louis and Daisy.

The news of Paul Kelly's death came as a relief to everyone. 'We think it was the wooden boxes that sank the cab so quickly,' explained Dick Tracker as he described the hundreds of dollar bills floating in the water when the cab had been pulled to the surface. 'We arrested his driver.'

Violet saw Louis swallow hard and hold Daisy's hand more tightly than ever. But it wasn't Louis she was worried about. It was Garth. Poor Garth, who had only just discovered that it was Paul Kelly behind his father's death, now had to understand that the man responsible would never be brought to justice. Garth's face was rigid. Violet knew he could feel her eyes on him but he didn't look up.

Dick Tracker cleared his throat. He had studied this case intensely since men from his detective agency had been brought in to guard Daisy Van Horn's portrait at Delmonico's, and he knew exactly who everyone in the room was. Lord Percy had instructed him to say what he had to say in front of everyone, but Lord Percy could not have known what Dick Tracker had been told barely half an hour before. He cleared his throat again.

'Uh, yeah, as I said, Kelly's driver, one Tortoise

Molloy, was arrested as soon he made it to the shore. He knew the game was up, of course, but he wanted to strike a deal.'

Lord Percy looked up as he realised that Dick Tracker had more than news of Paul Kelly's death to tell them, and he cursed himself for not listening when the detective had wanted to speak to him alone first.

At the same time as Lord Percy said, 'Excuse me, Mr Tracker.' Dick Tracker said, 'It concerns Philip Van Horn.'

Daisy started in her chair. 'He's dead, isn't he?' she said in a harsh voice.

Dick Tracker nodded. 'Yes, Miss Van Horn. I'm sorry to say he is.'

Mickey Gallagher bit his lip to stop himself from talking. He knew perfectly well what Kelly's orders would have been to his henchmen as soon as they picked up Philip Van Horn. It was the way Kelly always got rid of people who were bothering him but even Mickey understood that now would not be the time to speak.

'Did he have him drowned with a lump of

cement tied to his foot?' Garth's voice was so low, it was barely more than a growl.

Dick Tracker looked at the young man with the square face that was now crumpled with anguish. He knew who he was. The case of Conrad Hudson had been on their books for a long time and, while they suspected Kelly, they never had any proof. 'Yes, Garth,' said Dick Tracker in an even voice. He tried to hold the boy's eyes with his own. 'He suffered the same death as I suspect your father did. It was Kelly's trademark. We wouldn't have known where to find Van Horn if the driver hadn't told us.'

It was at that moment that Violet noticed Homer. He was sitting on the top of the curtain pole and, to her complete and utter horror, he held the same two Fabergé eggs in his paws. She gasped and her hands flew to her mouth.

Immediately Garth was beside her. 'I'm all right, Vi. Truly I am, you mustn't worry about me.' He patted her arm. 'It's more of a relief than anything else.'

Violet's eyes widened as she saw Homer looking

down at her. Now he was holding one egg with his foot and lightly throwing the other from paw to paw. Violet gasped again and opened her mouth to speak but nothing came out.

'Please don't be upset on my account,' cried Daisy Van Horn. She sat down on Violet's other side. 'In many ways, I've been expecting something like this to happen since the moment I first saw my father with Paul Kelly.' She paused and a look of pure weariness passed over her face. 'I'm not even sure if I care any more. Too many terrible things have happened.'

Homer couldn't understand why Violet hadn't called him. The last time he had come into this place with its funny smell and shiny things she had done exactly what he wanted. He decided to try something else. He hung from his tail and tossed the eggs between his paws and his feet at the same time.

Violet made a choking noise but not before Lady Eleanor, following Violet's gaze, let out a high-pitched shriek. She pointed limply to the curtain pole, then staggered towards the door and slumped onto the sofa.

Something like a French farce started all over again.

Garth, Daisy, Louis and Lord Percy believed that the ghastliness of the news had overwhelmed Violet and her mother. Dottie was called for and smelling salts were administered all round. Mickey, who had noticed Homer at the same time as Violet, could only guess that the painted gilt eggs in his paws were worth a lot of money and now that Homer was chattering angrily, something had to be done quickly.

'Talk to him,' squawked Violet. All the horror and tension of the day had built up inside her like lava in a volcano and she knew that any minute now she was going to burst into hysterical laughter.

'And just what would de munkey loik to hear?' Mickey cocked his head and looked up at Homer. 'Is it a bit of fresh air yer after?' he called in a playful, soothing voice.

Homer threw both eggs in the air and caught them neatly in his paws. He recognised that voice. He liked that voice. He ran up and down the curtain rail waiting to hear more.

'Percy!' cried Lady Eleanor in her most imperious voice. The smelling salts had worked their usual wonders. 'I will not tolerate that little beast a moment longer. *Do* something!'

Lord Percy looked around the room. Thanks to Homer, all the horror and sadness had gone from everyone's faces. Especially from Garth's and Daisy's. Now Garth was laughing with Mickey and Violet, while Daisy was staring adoringly at Louis. Even his beautiful wife looked more beautiful than ever, with a little colour in her cheeks. Lord Percy knew exactly what to do. He rang for more champagne and sent Dottie to fetch Herbert Wannamaker from his study.

Dick Tracker couldn't believe what was happening. He had heard stories of the peculiar behaviour of the English upper classes but he had never believed them. Now he knew they were all true.

Two weeks later, Violet swung up onto a high chrome stool in a Soda Fountain bar. It was the same place Garth had taken her to soon after their arrival in New York. As she stared down at the

215

shiny blue tiles on the floor she wondered if Louis and Daisy would be standing by the rails of the *SS Olympia* watching the blue sea below them. Or whether Herbert Wannamaker would be describing once more the secret he couldn't keep any longer. He had rented them an exquisite little apartment in a square just around the corner from Montmartre Cathedral.

Violet looked at the brand-new wristwatch she had insisted on buying against her mother's advice. It was so much more convenient than fiddling about looking for the one on a chain around her neck. The tiny hands said it was almost twelve o'clock. Any minute now, Mickey and Madame Poisson would arrive. Mickey had been taken to a tailor's shop on Fifth Avenue to be measured for a suit. It was Lord Percy's idea. *'My dear boy, you can't possibly be the head of a charity if you appear to be a charity case yourself.'*

Violet smiled to herself. She had never seen anything like the look of pure astonishment on Mickey's face when Garth and Louis had told him they were donating Van Horn's legacies to setting

216

up The Mickey Gallagher Charity for Homeless Boys. For a moment Violet had thought that Mickey was going to burst into tears.

Little did she know she was absolutely right. If Mickey hadn't had Homer on his shoulder to bury his face into, he would have bawled like a baby.

'A penny for your thoughts?' asked Garth, spinning the menu card in its chrome holder on the counter.

'A penny?' replied Violet. 'A hundred bucks at least.'

'OK. OK.' Garth knew what she was thinking about because he was thinking the same thing. 'Let's keep it simple then. Do you want to sneak in a three-scoop chocolate fudge soda before Mickey and codfish get here?'

Violet looked into Garth's bright-eyed face and grinned. 'Would I lie to you?'

THE DIAMOND TAKERS

The adventure begins to take shape . . .

'So what did they say?' Violet asked Garth outside the Ritz Hotel in Paris. Madame Poisson had left to go to her own quarters and it was the first chance they had to talk on their own. The porter opened the heavy glass doors and they walked into the vast entrance hall. A huge chandelier spread sparkling light over heavy gold chairs arranged around sumptuous Turkish rugs. Lilies were arranged on the polished surface of every sideboard and the air was thick with their scent. The Ritz was unlike any hotel Violet had ever known. It was more like staying in a grand French chateau.

'So what—?' began Violet again.

Beside her Garth froze. 'Shhh!'

Violet turned and followed his gaze. 'It's them!' she gasped.

Sure enough at the far end of the tiled marble floor, the man and woman who had been sitting on the Boulevard, were speaking rapidly to the manager of the hotel. They looked extremely upset. The woman's pale skin was flushed. She had taken off her red beret and kept running her hands through her short blonde hair. Beside her, her husband was drumming his fingers on his lapel as if trying to control his anger. A *gendarme* stood beside a skinny maid who was wiping her face with a rag of a handkerchief and staring unhappily at her feet.

'Quick,' whispered Garth. 'We'll hear more behind those palms!'

Violet and Garth walked quickly across the marble floor and sat down behind a clump of spiky leaves. As she watched Garth following every word of the conversation, Violet cursed herself for the hundredth time that day for not practising her French more often. Garth, on the other hand, had been Madame Poisson's star pupil and now spoke the language fluently.

All Violet could do was stare at the couple and catch what words she could. But at least Violet understood that the woman's diamonds had been stolen and that the maid had raised the alarm. At last the hotel manager turned to the *gendarme* and the two men left the hall, taking the maid with them.

Violet watched the woman's distraught face as she

walked with her husband towards the wide curving staircase. She appeared to be on the point of collapse. Then the two figures disappeared around a corner on the first floor.

'I misunderstood what they were saying on the Boulevard,' said Garth before Violet had time to ask. 'It was her mother's diamond choker that they were planning to take to the bank for safekeeping.' He was furious with himself for getting it wrong.

'Was anything else taken?' asked Violet feeling a twinge of pleasure at Garth's discomfort since he was always teasing her for being so slack with her own French.

'Almost all of her family's jewellery. Her mother died last month and Madame Duchamps—'

'Who's she?' asked Violet.

'That's the woman's name,' explained Garth. 'She's called Florence and he's called Henri.'

Violet tried not to show that her moment of pleasure had turned back into irritation. *She must try harder with her French.* 'Did the *gendarme* have any ideas about who might have stolen it?'

Garth shook his head. 'That's why the man was so angry. He had heard a rumour at the British Embassy last night that there were jewel thieves in the city. But the *gendarme* didn't know anything about it.'

221

'What about the hotel manager?'

Garth shook his head again. 'He hadn't heard anything either. Otherwise, he said he would have employed extra security guards in the hotel.'

Violet thought for a moment. 'Did the Duchamps inform the hotel that they had such valuable jewellery in their room?'

'Apparently, they wrote a letter to the concierge but it was never delivered.'

'So what happens next?'

'The policeman was sure that they would find the thieves soon. The choker is famous because of the pink diamond in the clasp so it would be very hard to sell.'

'I wonder if the maid would talk to us,' said Violet. She couldn't bring herself to say 'you'.

'Uh, uh.' Garth shook his head. 'This is one mystery someone else will have to solve. Like you said on the Boulevard, we're going to Monte Carlo tomorrow, and anyway the Duchamps have offered an reward of ten thousand francs.' He paused and shrugged. 'They're bound to get the choker back.'

Violet replied as she hadn't been listening. 'It would be fun to go to Monte Carlo with ten thousand francs in our pocket.'

'Violet!' cried Garth. 'I thought you disapproved of gambling!'

'Only when it's nothing but luck. Playing a good game of cards is different. That's a skill.'

'All the more reason to let someone else get the reward. I don't want your father accusing me of leading you astray.'

'But it was you who taught me how to play poker!' protested Violet. She touched his arm. 'You're just jealous because now I win every time.'

Behind her an enormous carriage clock chimed six o'clock.

'Oh, no!' cried Violet.

'What's wrong?'

'We have to meet my parents in fifteen minutes!' Violet stood up. 'Do me a favour and tell them I'll be fashionably late.'

Before Garth could say that Lady Eleanor was *so* fashionable, she always appeared at least half an hour after everyone else, Violet was running up the stairs, two steps at a time.

Twenty five minutes later, Violet stood in front of the long mirror in her bedroom. She had chosen a simple evening dress of finely striped black and turquoise silk taffeta. The hem and sleeves were edged with a plaited ribbon of black satin and sewn with tiny silver stars. Her hair was drawn back as smoothly as she could manage and held up with two ebony combs. A single strand of gleaming jet beads lay around her neck.

She pulled on a bolero jacket in a heavier turquoise silk and checked herself in the mirror for the last time. She was not a beauty like her mother but as she grew older she was beginning to learn that if she dressed simply she could make the best of her features which were handsome rather than pretty. Her mother was famous for her high cheekbones, sparkling blonde hair and pale green eyes. But Violet took after her father's side of the family. Her hair was dark and curly and she had a long face with a wide mouth. Her eyes, however, were the startling blue of lapis lazuli.

'Such lovely eyes,' Lady Eleanor would murmur. 'From my Irish side of the family, of course.' And if Lord Percy was in the room, he would agree with his wife and raise his eyebrows at Violet.

Violet fixed a pair of turquoise stud earring to her ears and gave the ebony combs a last push to hold them in place.

Then she picked up a silver evening purse and shut the door behind her.

'Violet! You look quite the thing, you really do!' Lady Eleanor Winters sat up in her chair and lifted her porcelain cheek for a kiss. As Violet bent down, her mother's perfume filled her nostrils. Lily of the Valley. It was always the same.

'Percy,' cried Lady Eleanor as Violet straightened and looked around the room for Garth. 'I do believe Violet should have a glass of champagne! We are in Paris after all!'

Lord Percy smiled in agreement and turned to his daughter. In Lord Percy's opinion, it was a blessing Violet was not a beauty like her mother and, for that matter, didn't share her mother's passion for clothes. Lord Percy knew Violet was determined to go to university and he was sure she would achieve her goal. He held out a glass of vintage champagne and raised his own towards her. 'You look lovely, my dear.'

'Thank you, father,' said Violet. 'I am having the most exciting time, already.' Violet sipped at her champagne and let the delicious bubbles fizz on her tongue. 'Have you seen Garth?'

'I presumed he spent the day with you and Madame,' replied Lord Percy.

For a moment, Violet was puzzled. It would only have taken Garth ten minutes to climb into his evening suit and stiff white collar. Why would he be so late?

At that moment, Garth came into the room. A huge lady dressed in a beaded grown with a spray of pink ostrich plumes attached to her elaborately piled hair walked beside him. Her bosom was almost entirely covered with pearls and she wore an enormous square cut diamond brooch on the neckline of her dress.

Violet almost cried out with delight. It was Mrs Stuyvesant Fish from New York, one of the few of her mother's friends that Violet actually liked. Garth must have met her in the hall. No wonder he had been late!

'Violet! My dear!' The great lady turned and beamed. 'How lovely to see you! As I was telling Garth, you are both still the talk of the town in New York!' She reached out a hand whose every finger sparkled with rings and touched Violet on the cheek. 'Now, tell me, how is that little monkey of yours? I did think he was absolutely adorable.'

Mrs Stuyvesant Fish's fondness for Violet's pet monkey was one of the reason Violet liked her so much. 'Homer's very well, thank you, but' – a shadow passed over Violet's face – 'I'm afraid he's not with me.'

'Why is that?' asked Mrs Stuyvesant Fish, frowning. 'A clever young monkey needs a change of scene. He would have *loved* Paris.' She paused. 'And now Garth tells me, you are off to Monte Carlo. Just the place for Homer, I would have said.'

'I'm afraid my mother thought differently,' replied Violet. 'Especially since that time in New York when he took the Fabergé eggs—'

'But he didn't *break* them!' interrupted Mrs Stuyvesant Fish. 'He was only curious. He *is* a monkey after all.' She looked across the room to Lady Eleanor, exquisite in a gown of sheer black silk embroidered with seed pearls. 'But you, of course, understand this.'

Violet had a sudden vision of Homer shut up in his cage in the nursery of her parents' London house. Her throat went tight. 'There was no convincing my mother,' she murmured.

'Then I shall introduce you to Toto.' Mrs Stuyvesant Fish patted Violet's arm. 'We all need fur in our lives, my dear.'

'Who's Toto?' asked Violet. As she spoke, Garth stepped forward. Against his black suit, Violet hadn't noticed the tiny black bundle what was nestling in his elbow.

It was a toy poodle puppy and this time, Violet did shriek with delight as Garth passed the tiny dog into her arms.

'There you are, my dear,' said Mrs Stuyvesant Fish. 'And what's more I have decided to come with you to Monte Carlo, tomorrow.' She smiled into Violet's flushed happy face. 'I shall need help looking after Toto.'

Later when Mrs Stuyvesant Fish had mentioned her

new plan, Lady Eleanor and Lord Percy were delighted. Their American friend had never been to Monte Carlo before and it would give Lady Eleanor a chance to pay her back for her kindness in New York.

Lady Eleanor patted Mrs Stuyvesant Fish lightly on the arm. 'Dear Gwendoline, I am imagining our days already! You *will* join us for dinner tonight, won't you? We are dining with the Grand Duke Michael and his wife Sophy and some friends of theirs who have just arrived in Paris this evening.' Lady Eleanor clapped her hands. 'It will be a thrilling party! You will be the envy of New York, I assure you!'

Mrs Stuyvesant Fish started to demur but that moment, Violet looked up and saw two fabulously-dressed women sweep into the room. They were followed by two men, both in elegant white tail coats and ties. One of the men was tall with a full beard. The other had red hair that stuck up in tiny spikes from his head.

With her unerring social instinct, Lady Eleanor turned just as the group was upon them and made introductions.

It appeared that the man with red hair was the Grand Duke, and the shorter, squatter of the two women was his wife Sophy, who made up for her shape with an elaborate silver ball gown. The tall man with the full beard was Count Drakensburg. Beside him, the Countess, whose hair was dark red, wore a necklace of emeralds over a low-cut fitted yellow gown trimmed with flounces of Belgian lace.

Once again, Lady Eleanor pressed Mrs Stuyvesant Fish to join their party, and this time she accepted, on the condition, she said smiling, that 'an old lady could be seated between the young ones.'

Two hours later, Violet watched as the Countess Drakensburg sipped delicately at a teaspoonful of sorbet flavoured with brandy. They were over half way through dinner and everyone appeared to be enjoying themselves. Everyone that is, except the Countess. Time and time again, Violet had had seen her turn from the Grand Duke on her right to speak across the table to Mrs Stuyvesant Fish who was talking to Garth, but somehow the right pause never occurred and she had to give up.

Violet sipped at the tangy sorbet. She remembered once listening with disbelief as Madame Poisson had explained how a sorbet was supposed to cut through the richness of an elaborate dinner (in this instance, salmon served with sauce hollandaise and roast goose stuffed with walnuts, refresh the taste buds) and restore the appetite for the courses still to come.

At the time Violet had thought it the strangest theory but now she knew that the right kind of sorbet did exactly what the codfish had said.

Suddenly there was a lull in the conversation and Violet saw the Countess put down her spoon.

'I understand you are staying in Paris for the rest of the week, Mrs Stuyvesant Fish,' she said warmly. 'We would be delighted if you would join us at the Opera tomorrow night.'

Mrs Stuyvesant Fish patted her mouth delicately with her damask napkin. 'How very kind of you, my dear Countess. And indeed, I would have so loved to come but only this evening, I decided to join Lord Percy and Lady Eleanor in Monte Carlo.' She smiled. 'It was a spur of moment decision, you understand.'

A strange expression flickered over the Countess's face. And as soon as it appeared, it went again. She looked down at the tablecloth, so that she wouldn't be tempted to stare.

'But you must stay another night,' insisted the Countess. 'Why, it's the last performance of *La Bohème* and we have reserved a box!'

'Surely not for me, Countess?'

Violet turned. There was a kind smile on Mrs Stuyvesant Fish's face but her eyes looked puzzled.

The Countess smiled in return and added lightly that

it was merely their custom to reserve a box for a final performance.

Immediately, the Count said something to Lord Percy and the two men laughed heartily. Then Garth asked Mrs Stuyvesant Fish about his friend Louis Cobolt who had come out to live in Paris.

'Gracious, what a daft old woman, I am!' Mrs Stuyvesant Fish put down her sorbet spoon. 'I've been meaning to tell you his news all evening.'

It appeared that the odd exchange between the Countess and Mrs Stuyvesant was forgotten. Then Violet saw the same expression flicker across the Countess's face and suddenly she recognised it.

For some extraordinary reason, the Countess was annoyed.

Violet didn't understand. Could it be that Mrs Stuyvesant Fish had forgotten about the arrangement. But that was impossible. She and the Countess had not met before. Then again, perhaps Violet had missed something that had taken place earlier. She looked down the length of the table glittering with silver candlesticks, and crystal, her mother sitting at the end like a queen presiding over her court, her shoulder-length diamond earrings flashing in the candlelight.

Suddenly Violet was tired. All the extraordinary things she had seen that day spun in her mind like so many pieces of coloured glass in a kaleidoscope. She stifled a yawn behind her hand.

At that moment, her mother rose. It was the signal for the ladies to withdraw and leave the gentlemen to their port and cigars. Violet stood up with Mrs Stuyvesant Fish.

'Will you excuse me,' she said in a low voice. 'I think I shall go to bed.'

Mrs Stuyvesant Fish smiled. 'Exactly, my intention, my dear. What with my new plans, I have many arrangements to make.'

Violet could feel eyes boring into her. She looked up just in time to see the Countess turn quickly away.

Violet felt a shiver of dislike and once again she had a strong feeling that something was going on that she didn't understand. But she pushed it to the back of her mind. Tomorrow, they were going to Monte Carlo and she would never see the Count and Countess again.

FOLLOW IN THE STEPS OF LADY VIOLET WINTERS...
by winning a weekend trip to Paris!
THE PRIZE: A weekend trip to Paris for one lucky entrant, a friend and an adult*

Includes:

- Return travel from London Waterloo to Paris by Eurostar
- Return minibus transfers to/from your hotel.
- 4 star hotel accommodation with breakfast
- A Seine river cruse
- A carnet of 10 Paris metro/bus per person

*trip is for 1 adult (parent or legal guardian of winner); and 2 children under the age of 12 on or before 31st December 2006. See over page for terms and conditions.

HOW TO ENTER: Simply write your name, address, email (where available) and date of birth on a postcard and answer the questions below (answers can be found in this book!).

IMPORTANT: Entries require parental consent – please ask your parent/guardian to name and sign your entry (entries without parental consent will be discarded).

- What was Homer doing when Violet found him in the drawing room of their house?

- What is the name of the gangster who runs the pet shop?

- Why does Garth go in disguise to the Silver Dollar with Mickey?

- What is Philip Van Horn's profession?

- Why did Paul Kelly kidnap Louis Colbolt?

- What is the name of Paul Kelly's driver?

SEND YOUR ENTRY TO: Lady Violet Competition, Simon and Schuster, Children's Marketing Department, Africa House, 64-78 Kingsway, London, WC2B 6AH

CLOSING DATE FOR ENTRIES: 30th June 2006

TERMS & CONDITIONS:

The prize consists of return travel from London Waterloo to Paris by Eurostar; Return minibus transfers to/from your hotel; 4 star hotel accommodation with breakfast; A Seine river cruise; a carnet of 10 Paris metro/bus per person; travel insurance. For 1 adult (parent or legal guardian of winner) and 2 children (both aged 12 and under on 31st December 2006). Travel to and from winner's home to London Waterloo not included. The weekend break must be taken before 31st December 2006 (excluding Christmas period and subject to availability).

Entrants must be aged no more than 12 years of age on or before 31st December 2006 and resident in the UK and supply evidence to this effect, should the promoter request it.

Only one entry per person.

One entry per household only.

Possession of passports and necessary documents to travel are the responsibility of the winner.

No purchase necessary – entry forms are available by post from: Marketing Department, Simon and Schuster Children's, Africa House, 64-78 Kingsway, London, WC2B 6AH. Please enclose a SAE.

To enter the competition each entrant must answer the 6 questions on a postcard/piece of paper which must also include the entrant's name, address, email (if available) date of birth and signature of parent/guardian.

Entries must be sent or delivered to Lady Violet Competition, Simon and Schuster, Children's Marketing Department, Africa House, 64-78 Kingsway, London, WC2B 6AH. Proof of posting will not be accepted as proof of receipt or entry.

The winner will be the entrant who has answered all 6 questions correctly drawn at random after the closing date.

Only entries properly completed and received by Simon and Schuster before the closing date will be entered into the competition.

Fraudulent, illegible, defaced or incorrectly competed entries will be disqualified.

All entries must be received by 5pm on 30th June 2006 ('the closing date')

By entering the competition the winners of any prize agree to participate in such promotional activities and feature in such promotional material as Simon and Schuster may require.

The panel of judges will be comprised of the Marketing Director of Simon and Schuster Children's Books, the Publisher of Simon and Schuster Children's Books and Karen Wallace, the author of the Lady Violet series.

No part of the prize is exchangeable for cash or any other prize.

The judge's decision is final and no correspondence will be entered into.

This competition is open to all residents of the UK and Eire, excluding employees of Simon and Schuster UK Ltd (the promoter of this competition) any subsidiary of Simon and Schuster UK Ltd or members of their immediate family.

Simon and Schuster Ltd has arranged this competition in good faith and do not accept any liability relating to the prize.

Winner will be notified by post by 31st July 2006.

Winner and results will be announced on 31st July 2006 and available on Simon and Schuster UK website: simonsays.co.uk

Promoter: Simon and Schuster UK Ltd, Africa House, 64-78 Kingsway, London, WC2B 6AH